RETURN TO YE...

The nurse wheeled Betty out of the house, then asked what part of the estate she'd like to visit. She hesitated, but knew that she could put it off no longer—no matter how much it would hurt.

"The quarry, Maggie," she said, determined. It was time to shake this ghost haunting her memory—the memory still only partially healed.

The ground sloped downward as they neared the edge of the quarry. Suddenly the workmen set off an explosion. The nurse screamed in sudden fright, and let go of the wheelchair. It began to roll towards the edge of the quarry. Betty tried to stop it, but the momentum was too great. The wheels burned the skin from the palms of her hands, and she knew that she was about to die . . .

**PUT PLEASURE IN YOUR READING
Larger type makes the difference**
This EASY EYE Edition is set in large, clear type—at least 30 percent larger than usual. It is printed on non-glare paper for better contrast and less eyestrain.

Dorothy Daniels
The Marble Angel

LANCER EASY EYE EDITIONS

LANCER BOOKS
NEW YORK

A LANCER BOOK

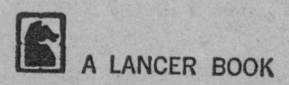

THE MARBLE ANGEL
Copyright © 1970 by Dorothy Daniels
All rights reserved
Printed in the U.S.A.

LANCER BOOKS, INC. • 1560 BROADWAY
NEW YORK, N.Y. 10036

ONE

I felt more alone at that moment than I had ever felt in my eighteen years of life. Seated in my wheelchair, to which I'd been wedded for almost two years, I rolled along the wide, deserted corridor of the main floor of the large Boston hospital which had been my home for eighteen months. Prior to that I'd spent six months in a Rutland hospital where they finally admitted they had done all they could for me. The Boston hospital had taken eighteen months to reach the same conclusion. I was now on my way to see the Chief of Staff and then I'd be passed on into the hands and tender care of my cousin Lew Hutching and his wife Rena. I cared little about going home —I suppose because I considered my life over but I'd endured all the idleness I could and so I decided my days of emptiness might seem less so were I to apply myself diligently to the business left me by my parents. Papa had talked with me often and at great length concerning the many facets of it and though, since the accident, I'd suffered a lapse of memory, it seemed that, from time to time, words, phrases and terms of the work would slip into my mind.

Dr. Beardsley was elderly and kind, but inclined

to be brusque. I didn't know then that it was the best way to handle patients such as me. He wore his usual long white coat and his usual benign expression as I wheeled myself into his office and stopped the chair directly in front of his desk.

"How are you this morning, Betty?" he asked.

My eyes rebuked him. "A bit weary. I overdid it last night, dancing every dance. Not retiring until dawn."

"Oh, come now. No need to develop that vein of sarcasm you've uncovered in yourself."

I said, "I feel like a convict leaving prison and you're the warden giving me last bits of advice. Please, Dr. Beardsley, don't procrastinate. Without wishing to be rude—for I know you've done everything possible for me—I'm eager to start my journey."

"Good," he said, and became the eminent doctor he was. "Yes, we have done everything possible for you. You understand your condition as well as we. You're paralyzed from the waist down and it's possible you will not recover the use of your legs. That's a brutal way to put it, but I think you rather like brutality when it comes to your condition."

"I dislike rudeness of any kind, for any reason."

"You're young and attractive," he went on, ignoring my rebuff. "You have the advantage of wealth and you have relatives who've shown great concern over your condition. What happened was an accident, but you choose to blame yourself and whether you realize it or not, you're pleased that you are now a cripple. It softens the blame you assign yourself because of the deaths of your parents in the same accident."

"The accident was caused by my carelessness," I retorted.

"I don't agree. If your mental attitude was different, there's a chance you might recover, but because of your guilt complex—you've resigned yourself to being an invalid. Try to accept what has happened and forget your self-blame which is turning you into a bitter young woman or you'll put a blight on your whole life."

I lowered my gaze, for his eyes seemed to penetrate into the deepest reaches of my mind. "My life is over."

"If you choose to make it so. I prefer to think that though your condition will put restrictions on you, your life can still be full and useful. But you will have to be the one to make it so. I'm sorry we were unable to convince you."

I knew I was behaving childishly, but I could not accept his logic. "You did everything possible."

"Yes, we did," he replied. "I only wish you'd seen fit to cooperate with us."

He arose, came around his desk and placed a comforting hand on my shoulder. "The advice I just gave you is the only medicine which will help you. One thing more—when your self-pity consumes you, think of people who can't speak, or see, or move a muscle, people who have no money, no friends, no relatives to help ease their pain and forget their hours of loneliness."

"I'm sorry I was such a bad patient," I said. "Thank you for everything. Good-by, Doctor."

"Write me, Betty. I'd like to see you lick this. I believe you have the backbone to do it."

"I'll write," I said. I had no intention of doing so

and he knew it, but he nodded as if pleased.

He followed me to the door where a nurse waited to wheel me to the ambulance entrance. There, a driver in a hired carriage had maneuvered his horses as close to the receiving platform as possible so I could be transferred from the wheelchair to the vehicle with the greatest possible ease for them and a minimum of discomfort for me. Waiting for me were Lew and Rena. I hadn't seen them in weeks and the sight of familiar faces was helpful to my spirits. I smiled and waved as I was rolled closer.

We exchanged warm greetings, then Lew took charge. He was thirty, while Rena was five years younger. Her hair was almost jet black and her brown eyes sparkled with a liveliness born of a *joie de vivre*. Though Lew was her true love, she enjoyed mild flirtations, for she was well aware of her beauty and superb figure. She was also cognizant that she and Lew drew all eyes when they were together, for his handsomeness matched her beauty. He was, truly, a blond Adonis—tall, muscular and possessed of infinite charm.

I felt a sense of guilt, regarding them, for I envied them their obvious good health and, I suppose, their happiness. I knew that, despite Rena's overwhelming desire for masculine admiration, their love for each other was genuine and all encompassing. Her boundless energy and vivaciousness couldn't help but make her irresistible to the opposite sex. Lew knew it and was most tolerant about it. He, in turn, could have made many a feminine eye turn his way, yet he was devoted to her.

Yes, I was guilty of jealousy regarding their happiness. To my mind, they had everything and I had nothing. Nothing except a broken body which I thoroughly deserved.

Lew issued commands to the carriage driver so that, between them, they lifted me from the chair and deposited me gently on the back seat of the carriage. In moments we were on our way to the railroad depot for the journey to Rutland, Vermont. From there it was a long carriage ride to where I lived. Now that the journey was under way, I wished it would take forever. Going home was going to be an agonizing process for me and I wished suddenly to be back in the hospital.

As the carriage rattled over the cobblestone streets of Boston, I did take some interest in looking about, studying the fashions and thinking that my dress was already out of style, though it made little difference. I reminded myself that nobody looks at the manner in which a crippled young lady dresses.

Rena broke into my reverie with her usual enthusiasm. "Wait until you see the pretty paper decorating the walls of your bedroom. It has dainty pink roses on a pale blue background. I swear the blue matches that of your eyes."

"I have no intention of occupying my room upstairs," I said testily. "I wrote, stating the room downstairs I wished to be refurbished for my convenience."

"And it was done," Lew said. "But only at my insistence."

"Why should you have to insist when the house happens to be mine?" I disliked having to call attention to the fact, but I also disliked my suggestions to be ignored.

"Please don't get touchy about it, Betty," Rena

implored, pouting prettily. "We thought you'd be happier upstairs."

"Just how did you expect me to get up and down the stairs?"

She eyed me hopefully. "There are enough men around who could carry you."

I stiffened with anger. "I wouldn't countenance such a thing. I don't wish to discuss it further except to state that, from now on, when I say I want something done, I'll expect my wishes to be carried out."

Rena sighed. "Dr. Beardsley said you were very . . ."

"Difficult?" I asked.

"No," Lew offered. " 'Touchy' was the word he used. I don't blame you, Betty. Rena didn't like the idea of your bedroom downstairs, but, as you say, it's your house. Make that plain when you get home. If you don't, you'll end up believing you're a guest and perhaps an uninvited one."

I smiled, despite myself. "Forgive me for being feisty. I'll admit I'm not easy to get along with."

"If you're not, you've changed," Lew said, chuckling. "You were a damn mischievous kid, but lovable, too. Pretty much of a tomboy. You'd rather run than walk. Not the least bit genteel."

I closed my eyes, as if by doing so, I could shut out the word picture he'd conjured up. "Please don't remind me of it."

His voice took on an apologetic tone. "I'm sorry. I didn't mean to stir memories."

I leaned forward and gave his hand, resting on the back of the seat, a reassuring pat. "I know you didn't. But if I had walked in a ladylike manner the day of the accident, instead of running like a hoyden, Mama and Papa would be alive."

I looked down at my limbs, grateful their uselessness was hidden behind the full skirt.

"Betty," Rena said, her warm brown eyes looking troubled, "you must stop blaming yourself. Dr. Bearsley said there's a chance of recovery."

"Very remote," I replied tonelessly.

"Even the fact that it's remote should give you hope," she argued.

"Don't you suppose in the loneliness of my hospital room, I tried to walk? Even stand?" I asked. "I fell several times."

"I'm sorry," she said. "Had I known, I'd never have mentioned it."

"No one knew. But I did try. And each time I fell, it seemed to take me hours to pull myself back onto the bed."

Lew gave me an encouraging smile. "At least it showed you still have spirit."

My smile was bitter. "I wouldn't advise you to wager any money on the degree of it. Let's not pursue this topic further. How are Aunt Liz and Uncle Elijah?"

Rena said, "Very important since they've assumed the running of the household. At least, Aunt Liz has. They're looking forward to seeing you."

My smile was reflective. "Is she as overwhelming as ever?"

"More so," Lew said. "She'd boss us if we gave her half a chance."

"And how are things going at the quarry?" I asked.

11

Lew said, "Splendidly. Reggie Mandaray is still the foreman and very conscientious. Dudley Seaver handles the books and complains if we steal a postage stamp or two. Harley Denison oversees the whole works and keeps in touch with our customers. It's a fine operation and runs like an expensive, beautifully-cared-for clock. You have nothing to worry about."

Nothing, I thought bitterly. Only that I was not able to walk and would never stand erect again. Only that I'd never know the love of a man, or hear the laughter of a child, or know the joy of comforting a tearful one, for I'd never inflict my useless body on anyone. Never to do anything but sit . . . and sit . . . and sit. I shut out the thoughts, for it brought tears to my eyes.

"Last month we ran into a sizeable section of saccharoidal marble," Lew went on. "It's got a bluish tinge and red veins and it cuts well. Harley says it'll sell for premium prices all over the world."

My interest was immediately aroused. "I shall look forward to seeing it."

"Don't tell me," Rena said, "you want to go near that ugly old quarry."

"I do—very much," I said. "I intend to involve myself deeply in the running of it."

Rena was shocked. "You could get killed down there. And after what happened to you . . ."

"Rena," Lew cautioned her to silence.

"It will be difficult," I admitted, "to see it for the first time. It will bring back a rush of bitter memories. Perhaps that's good since my memory still isn't all it should be. But it's coming back fast."

"I don't approve," Rena said. "After that horrible

tragedy, I believe I'd rather have a marker over my grave made of wood, to one of marble."

"Sacrilege," Lew replied dryly, "when you say that to the owner of one of the biggest marble quarries in the world."

Lew's attempt at humor did lift my spirits. But they were dashed when I was transferred to the pullman, for I was, once again, placed in a wheelchair to get me aboard and I was overwhelmed by my helplessness. I was relieved when the train pulled out and I was able to stare out of the window as the crowded Boston area quickly vanished and I saw once more the wonderful New England countryside to which I had been born. At least, I had my vision and my eyes greedily drank in its beauty.

I grew tired of Rena's well-meaning chatter and pretended to doze. The monotonous click-click of the rails did lull me into a sort of stupor, not truly asleep nor yet awake, but a state in which I could think and remember, especially that awful day at the rim of the quarry when the worlds of my father and mother ceased to exist, and my own turned into a nightmare. Often, in the hospital, I would dream about it and awaken with an ear-splitting scream as the horror came back.

I tried to think as Dr. Beardsley had advised. That there were many people far less fortunate than I. It was true. I had more money than I could use, a very large and wonderful home, relatives and friends. I could hear and speak. I could see and smell and taste. I could lose myself in the business of running the quarry. At least my days would be filled and I had a staff of faithful people who would help.

I opened my eyes and began a conversation in the lightest possible vein. In that manner the hours went by and, as we neared Rutland, I saw the passing scene grow familiar to me. The stone houses, the endless stone fences, the apple orchards, the quaint little towns that flashed by as the steam train puffed its way north. By the time we reached the depot, I was reasonably calm.

TWO

Lew picked me up and whispered that I should be ashamed of myself for gaining so much weight even though I hadn't gained an ounce. When he stepped off the car, with me still in his arms, Dudley Seaver was standing on the platform, looking much like a sentinel, with one hand resting on a wheelchair which had floral-patterned chintz cushions for both the seat and back.

His lean face widened in a smile of greeting. "Welcome home, Betty."

"Thank you, Dudley," I said. I attempted a smile, but my mouth twisted grotesquely, for the mere sight of him brought a flood of memories back—both happy and tragic. A sob did escape my throat, but once in my wheelchair, I gripped the arms tightly and thus brought my emotions under control. I knew then how difficult my days would be and how I must exercise every bit of will power I possessed to keep from thinking about myself. I was more determined than ever to lose myself in helping to run the quarry. I couldn't take over completely, for I wasn't well enough versed in it. Even if I were, I wouldn't dispense with the services of any of the three men who had done so much to make the quarry the success it was. I needed them, but I wanted to be a part of the operation. I had to be if I were to retain my sanity.

Dudley and Lew placed me in the back seat of the carriage. There was an afghan which Lew started to place about my knees, but I disdained it, laying it on the seat alongside. It was a warm summer day, even for Vermont. Dudley placed my luggage and wheelchair in a wagon which stood before the carriage. Obviously, he'd tethered the horse and wagon onto the carriage when he came to the village to meet us. Now he'd precede us back so that the wheelchair would be awaiting me on my arrival. It was obvious, particularly since Lew made a little ceremony of filling his pipe with tobacco, tamping it down just so with his fingers, then searching his pockets in a pretense of seeking matches. I suppose I should have been pleased at his little game of subterfuge, but it only served to annoy me. I was not a child and didn't need to be humored. It was only with difficulty I refrained from suggesting we get started.

Finally we did, but at a leisurely pace. I didn't mind that, for I disliked being jostled and the three-mile ride gave me a chance to compose myself. I would not let my emotions overwhelm me again. Apparently Lew and Rena were aware that this was a trying time for me and neither attempted to engage me in conversation.

I must admit the sweetness of the air, the fresh greenness of the shrubbery and trees, the birds trilling their songs in the branches as we passed, sent a feeling of exuberance through me I'd not experienced since before the accident.

The road finally approached the quarry. I could hear the work going on below and though we were not close enough to the overhang to see anything, I recognized the sound of the steam-driven rock drills. Particularly, the banging of the channeling machines as they cut into the floor of marble at the base of the quarry. I closed my eyes tightly as we came to a curve in the road where green turf ran to the edge of the steep cliff. That was where it had happened and I wasn't prepared to look at the scene again. Not quite yet.

We rounded a curve then and lost sight of the quarry, but were met by another sight, magnificent in its grandeur. It was the home I'd left two years before. Christened Bowen's Castle by the natives, it, indeed, resembled one, with myriad towers and battlements and deeply-recessed windows. It was constructed of marble taken from the quarry and, with the sun on it now, its beauty was breathtaking.

The sight of it brought a catch in my throat, for I'd known much happiness there. Perhaps too much, for my parents had indulged me and had given me generously of their love. And I had repaid that love . . . I caught myself up. If Dr. Beardsley were seated beside me and could read my mind, he would tell me in that benign way of his that I was, once again, indulging in self-pity. But I didn't see how blaming myself for an accident caused by my carelessness, was indulging in self-pity. I deserved to lose the use of my limbs. It was my punishment. I would learn to live with it, but I would do my best to atone for my sin by making the Bowen quarry the most well-known in the world.

I regarded the great expanse of lawn, the beautifully manicured shrubs, the tall, well-cared-for trees and the path, which led to the rear of the estate and continued on to the quarry.

I was gifted with excellent eyesight and I noted everyone on the porch waiting to greet me. It would be an ordeal, but one I was determined to meet. I made out the figures of Aunt Liz Pauley, Mama's sister, and her husband Elijah, handsome as a stage idol. Beside them stood Reggie Mandaray, the foreman of the firm. He was of middle age, a modest, unassuming man whose sole interest was his home and his job. To his right stood Harley Denison, general manager of the quarry and easily topping six feet. He was blessed with a strong, muscular body and rugged features which suggested an inner determination and strength. His manner seemed stern until he smiled and then his features softened, for he even smiled with his eyes. He was about thirty-five, but looked younger.

I recognized Lorette who managed the household and had two servants come in by the day. She could never keep them very long, for she was very demanding, but the castle was spotless, so Mama had put up with her tyrannical manner. I noticed one unknown face among those waiting to greet me. A tall woman of indeterminate years, wearing a white uniform.

"Who's the stranger?" I asked.

"Her name is Maggie Morfit," Rena said. "She's to look after you."

"Why wasn't I consulted?" I asked.

"Please don't be difficult, Betty," Rena pleaded. "You know you need someone."

"True," I admitted. "But I intended Lorette assist me until I found someone suitable."

"We only meant to be helpful," Rena said plaintively.

Of course they did, I thought. And I did need someone. It was just the idea of them taking matters into their own hands I resented. But I warned myself not to be difficult on my homecoming.

"Very well," I said. "But, from now on, please remember I'm the mistress of the Castle and I expect to be consulted on any plans which concern the running of it."

"Yes, Betty." Rena spoke politely, though I sensed her inner resentment.

"Don't be too hard on Rena," Lew said. "No one really hired Maggie. She came one day and asked if she might serve you. She's strong and healthy and willing. Also experienced."

"Who is she?"

"She lives in the village and she's a combination midwife and practical nurse."

"But why did she wish to serve me?" I was puzzled.

Rena said, "You might as well tell her, Lew."

"Her husband Tom was killed in an accident in the quarry three years ago," he said. "She said she was bitter at first, but as time went on, she realized it was his fault. Then you had this accident. She feels you're worse off than her husband was."

"What does she mean by that?" I persisted.

"That you're doomed to a life in the wheelchair," Rena said. "She thinks that's worse than being dead."

"Is she pleased about it?" I asked, still not certain as to the woman's motives.

"Good heavens, no," Rena exclaimed. "She remembers you. She said you were so filled with life —always a pleasant, friendly smile on your face and you reminded her of a little princess. In fact, that's what she keeps calling you—the princess."

"I don't feel like a princess and I hope you will tell her in private she is not to address me as such."

"I will," Rena said wearily. "Just try to be tolerant with us. I don't blame you for being bitter. You've paid a terrible price for what you did, but remember, none of the rest of us had anything to do with it."

"That's enough, Rena," Lew said sternly. "Betty has every right to be heartsick and bitter. And it's our duty to keep her spirits up."

"No, it isn't," I contradicted. "I'm behaving very pettishly. I know it. It's going to take me awhile to adjust. I only hope I can."

I could well imagine Rena silently agreed, but wisely refrained from making further comment. I believe all three of us felt a sense of relief when Lew halted the horse before the steps.

The next instant Harley Denison was down the step and, with one foot on the step of the carriage, he planted a kiss on my cheek and lifted me into his arms.

"About time you came home," he said, smiling in that devilish way of his. "I'm impatient to come a-courtin' you."

I laughed, despite myself. "You haven't changed, Harley. Still eager to pretend you're overwhelmed by whichever young, unattached female you happen to be near."

"Now, Betty," he chided, "you know I'm not like that."

"I know you are," I said. "And you know I know it. So behave yourself."

The tableau on the porch watched politely as he pretended dismay. "We'll pursue this topic later."

"I'll have a lot of time to discuss it with you."

"I'll make an appointment."

"That won't be necessary. Just look about for the wheelchair."

Dudley came around the house wheeling the chair. I was relieved to see it. He guided it onto the porch and stood alongside it, once again reminding me of a sentinel on guard duty.

Harley carried me up the steps and set me gently in the chair. He dropped his jocular manner and said, "Thank God, you're back. You'll warm the marble halls with your presence."

"Thank you, Harley. I'll make every effort."

"That's the right spirit, my dear," Aunt Liz said. She looked very regal in a purple satin tea gown. Though her face was unlined, she was of middle age, but still gave evidence of the beauty which was hers as a young girl. Mama had often spoken of it. Aunt Liz and Mama had been sisters, with Aunt Liz the older by several years. But she stood ramrod straight and her snow-white hair glistened in the sun from daily brushings.

She embraced me, then stepped back for Uncle Elijah to express his greetings. His face was deeply lined from his years spent outdoors, for he was a fishing and hunting enthusiast. His faded blue eyes crinkled at the corners when he smiled and his laugh was hearty, reminding me of Papa's.

He kissed me on the cheek, then eyed me critically. "About time you came back, honey. Place has been pretty dreary without you."

Reggie Mandaray came forward next. He nodded awkwardly. "Glad to have you home, Miss Betty."

He smiled with pleasure when I extended a hand. "I'm glad to be home and see all of you. How nice to see you too, Lorette."

"Thank you, Miss Betty," she said, making a slight curtsy. "I hope you'll find everything to your liking."

"I hope so too," Aunt Liz said, giving her a tart look. "I never saw anyone who hired and fired as fast as Lorette. I declare if she doesn't stop, no one will come to the Castle to work."

"In that case, I'll do it myself," she replied primly.

Uncle Elijah said, "Then you'd better put on a few pounds or you'll be a walking skeleton. With this mausoleum, you could stand a corps of workers."

"I manage nicely, sir," she said, giving no quarter.

"You do indeed," Uncle Elijah agreed. "Only thing is, whenever I see you moving along the hall pursuing the servants in that half run of yours, I expect you to be cracking a horsewhip. I think mentally you are."

Lorette's features never changed at Uncle Elijah's good-natured joshing. If she had her choice of a family coat of arms, I believe she'd select a mop and broom crossed over a pail. She was much too thin, probably from driving herself, but she was wiry and apparently very strong.

Then there was Gildy, the cook. She looked the part, for she was greatly overweight and seemed to be bursting out of her white uniform with oversize apron. But she was a warmhearted person as evidenced by her apple-cheeked smile.

"I'm looking forward to your cooking again," I told her.

"Thank you, Miss Betty," she replied. "I got your favorite for supper—roast beef with natural gravy."

"And heaps of those fluffy mashed potatoes, I hope," I said.

"Indeed, yes," she said. "All you wish."

I caught her hand and brought it to my cheek. "It's good to be back," I said. And strangely, I knew I meant it.

"Good to have you back, Miss."

Aunt Liz, with a wave of her hand, urged Maggie Morfit over. "Maggie has offered her services. She's quite competent. Brought recommendations which we've checked."

"So Rena told me," I said, studying the woman who stood before me. "Why do you wish to work for me, Mrs. Morfit?"

"Please call me Maggie, Miss Betty," she said. I was astounded that a woman as big and strong as she appeared had a voice and smile which matched in gentleness.

"Very well, Maggie," I said. "Please answer my question."

"It ain't too easy to put into words, but it's just that I felt great bitterness after my Joseph died. I felt your papa was responsible, though he denied it, blaming it on my Joseph's weakness for the bottle. However, I was given compensation. But then, when I saw what happened to your parents and how you're chair-confined, I realized accidents could happen to anyone. I'm ashamed for feeling bitterness in my heart toward you and your mama and papa. I'm sorry for what happened to them and to you."

"Thank you, Maggie," I said. "But it still isn't clear in my mind the point you're trying to make."

"I ain't got the education to express myself good," she said apologetically. "So I'll say it this way. When we sin, we should do penance of some sort to show the Almighty we're sorry. I want to do penance."

I was astounded and showed it.

"Please don't take offense, Miss Betty. I don't mean it that way. As I said, I ain't got the education to say what's in my mind. I want to work for you—without pay."

"I wouldn't countenance such a thing," I said.

I thought for a moment she was going to cry. "I'm sorry, Miss Betty. I wanted to work for you so bad."

She turned to go back inside. I suppose to change to her regular clothes. I reached out and stayed her with my hand.

"Maggie, I'll be glad to have you attend me—but only as a hired nurse. I will pay you."

"It ain't necessary, Miss."

"It's quite necessary, in my opinion. That is the only condition under which you may stay."

"If I have no choice," she said in that quiet way of hers, "I'll agree to your terms."

"Then let's get started. Please wheel me inside."

She did so and it was obvious from the care exercised with the chair, she was experienced. I felt I'd been a little too severe on Rena, rebuking her for having hired Maggie without consulting me. I already felt quite fortunate to have such a competent woman. I was also touched by her humility.

THREE

Once inside, the past seemed to rise up and close in on me, like a vise squeezing my heart. I saw Mama, once again descending the grand staircase, dressed in a beautiful green velvet gown which complimented her auburn hair. Her manner of movement was so graceful it seemed as if she floated rather than walked. And her laughter was as gay and light as her manner. And I saw Papa, awaiting her at the foot of the stairs, his arms extended to enclose her, his eyes drinking in her beauty and openly adoring her, as was I who stood beside him. After they embraced, their arms enclosed me, assuring me their love for me equaled that which they bore each other. And I heard again Papa's deep, hearty laughter, reverberating through the corridors and the high-ceilinged stairwell. How I wished they both still occupied the house. In that moment, I once again wished for death, as I had so many times in the hospital. I wondered why it couldn't have been I who'd met sudden death, shocking in its horror.

I pressed my back firmly against the back of the chair and directed Maggie to wheel me into the drawing room. Despite the warmth of the day, the house was chill. But Lorette had a fire going in the fireplace and Maggie wheeled me close to it, turning me around to face Aunt Liz and Uncle Elijah who had followed me into the room. Beyond them, the others lingered in the enormous hall.

I addressed Aunt Liz. "Please ask Rena and the men to come into the drawing room. I wish to speak to all of you to tell you why I returned."

Surprise etched her features, but she made no comment. When they filed in, I bade them draw chairs close so they too could enjoy the warmth emanating from the huge fireplace. Once they were seated, I lost no time in stating my plans.

"As you know, I have lost all use of my legs. From this point on, I will never again refer to the fact I shall never walk and I will appreciate it if each of you will also refrain from doing so. However, in order to take my mind off my affliction, I have come home to assist Harley in running the quarry."

"That's preposterous," Aunt Liz exclaimed. "You mustn't even think of such a thing. I'm in thorough disapproval of it."

"Fortunately, Aunt Liz, I don't need your approval."

She was stunned by my apparent boldness. "What has got into you?"

"An overwhelming desire to lose myself in work so I'll forget the fact that I'm confined to a wheelchair."

Harley said, "I'm in favor of it. Betty's as sharp mentally as ever."

"If you mean tart-tongued," Aunt Liz retorted, "she is indeed."

"I don't mean any such thing," he disputed, softening his words with a smile. "I like spirit in a woman.

While Betty was gifted with her mother's good looks, she has her father's resourcefulness."

"I do not believe John Bowen would have approved of his daughter getting involved in the machinations of the quarry. Nor would her mother, who also happened to be my sister."

"Aunt Liz, please don't upset yourself," I said.

"How can I help it?" She dabbed at her eyes with a handkerchief. "You're my care, my responsibility. If you go near that quarry, you might get killed. You're completely helpless, you know."

"Physically, yes," I admitted. "Not mentally."

"You suffered a complete loss of memory after the accident," she said remindfully.

"Dr. Beardsley said it was partially psychological. I didn't want to think of it. I still don't. But he explained my behavior by saying once I knew my parents were dead, I thrust all memory of that horrible day from my mind. Perhaps if I hadn't, I might be walking today."

"Is there hope, Betty?" Uncle Elijah said.

"No," I said firmly.

"That's not true," Rena said. "Dr. Beardsley said there was a remote chance you might regain the use of your legs."

"I don't care what Dr. Beardsley said," I retorted. "I tried to stand. I tried to walk. Each time I slid to the floor."

"I knew nothing about that," Aunt Liz said.

"I never told anyone until today. I tried several times to stand in my hospital room when I was alone. I'd ease myself over the side of the bed, holding on to the head of it. When I let go, I had to grab the mattress. Even then, I couldn't hold myself up. Now I want no more talk of that. Harley, you seem willing to work with me. I'll need your cooperation."

He said, "Be assured, you have it."

Dudley Seaver smiled and nodded. "If you feel well enough to do it, I'm all in favor, Miss Betty. All in favor."

Reginald Mandaray nodded his approval. "I'll cooperate in every way possible."

I smiled my thanks. "I will want you to bring all the books in a day or so and explain them to me, Dudley."

"Be glad to, Miss Betty," he said.

"I'm sure you know I have a good working knowledge of the quarry. Papa had hoped for a son, but once it was evident Mama could have no more children, he taught me a great deal about marble. He knew that one day I would inherit and it would be to my advantage to be informed regarding the business. I'm sure that much of what I've forgotten will come back, once I make a visit there and talk with my," I made a motion with my hand to encompass Harley, Dudley and Reggie, "cohorts."

Harley said, "Did Lew tell you we came upon a saccharoidal run? It's a deep blue and fantastically beautiful."

"Very unusual—and valuable," Reggie said.

"Yes, he did," I replied. "When will you undercut it?"

"As soon as possible," Reggie said.

"Splendid," I said in approval. "We must see to it that those who appreciate fine marble will be supplied with the best we can produce."

Harley said, "We'll work with you closely and follow your orders to the letter."

"Be assured, Harley, I shall consult you on everything. After all, I don't propose to run the quarry."

He smiled. "At least, not right away. But if I must work for a lady, I can't think of anyone I'd rather it be than you."

I nodded gratefully. "I appreciate your not resenting my desire to be a part of the operation. Be assured, I'll not overrule any suggestion you make unless I'm certain I'm right."

"Thank you, Betty," Harley said. "And now, I must beg your indulgence and get down to the quarry. With both Reggie and me away from there, some problem might come up which could prove unanswerable."

"Of course," I said. "Thank you for taking time from work to welcome me home. And thank you, Dudley, for bringing my chair to the station. It's far less humiliating than to be carried."

"I resent that," Lew said in good-natured banter. "I thought I did rather well."

"You did," I said. "It's just that I resent my helplessness."

"From the spirit you've just displayed," Harley said, "I don't believe a person in the room thought about your handicap until you just referred to it."

I smiled my appreciation. "A few words like that each day will do wonders to boost my morale."

"I'll see that you get them," Harley said, rising.

After the three men left, I addressed Aunt Liz. "I'm wearied by my travels and I'd like to rest."

"Of course, my dear," she said. "We brought your

bedroom furniture down, as you requested, and it's in the room adjoining the den."

"Please take me there, Maggie. I assume you know where it is."

"I do, Miss," she replied, already wheeling me toward the door.

"Please excuse me," I said to the others.

"I'll go with you," Aunt Liz said, "though I won't linger. I just want to know if everything is suitable."

"If it isn't," I said, smiling, "Lorette will see to it."

"I know that," Aunt Liz retorted. "I don't know how your mama ever put up with her."

"I suppose because whatever Lorette does, it is with us in mind."

Aunt Liz gave grudging praise. "She certainly earns her wages. But I may as well tell you she and I battle constantly."

We left the wide corridor and entered what had been Papa's den. The walls were lined with books and the small-paned, diamond-shaped, latticed windows glittered with colored light, for half the quarrels were of opaque colored glass. There was a serenity in the room, brought about by the deep leather chairs and couch which sat to one side of the fireplace. A large desk flanked the other side.

Maggie wheeled me through a door into a medium-sized room. Papa had had it furnished as a bedroom, for he often worked at the quarry until a late hour and didn't wish to enter the upstairs bedroom and disturb Mama's sleep. But his furniture was of dark wood, massive and very masculine. I liked the white and gold finish of mine, with its delicate lines. It was very feminine and Mama had selected it for me on my fifteenth birthday. Each time I looked at it

I would think of her. And that was what I wanted. A constant reminder of her and Papa. These two rooms would serve that purpose. Everything was exactly as I wanted it.

But there was one thing missing. A small Bible which I kept on a large casement window in my room. Since I wished to question Aunt Liz about Maggie, I asked the latter to go upstairs for it.

"What was the accident Maggie's husband was involved in?" I asked, once I knew she was out of hearing.

Aunt Liz countered my question with another. "Don't you remember a boiler blowing up at the quarry about three years ago?"

"Now that you mention it, I do—but only vaguely."

"Maggie's husband Joseph was killed in that explosion."

"Does she have children?"

"Neither kith nor kin. She's a hard worker and was in demand in the village both in caring for the sick and as a midwife. But once Joseph died, she became almost a recluse. Of course, she brooded and admits it. She came to us, as you now know, and actually pleaded to be allowed to care for you."

"I'm glad she did," I said. "I'll pay her extra. It's the least I can do."

"Your papa took good care of her, though the responsibility was not his. He'd dismissed Joseph Morfit several times because of coming to work intoxicated. But each time Joseph prevailed on him to let him return. I suppose because, when sober, he was a good worker."

"Well, I'm grateful for Maggie Morfit."

"I'm glad, my dear, because there isn't another

soul in the village available for this kind of work. Maggie's big and strong and willing. Your troubles are over."

Yes, I thought bitterly, my troubles are over. No more will I have to think about being lonely, trapped in a wheelchair, with a racking memory of screams and hurtling rock and sudden death.

Aunt Liz left me then and Maggie returned. I was heartened by the sight of the Bible she carried. Perhaps, in some way, that might help restore my courage. For I knew, despite the compliments I'd smilingly accepted from Harley, my spirit and my courage were a facade to hide the fact that I was a very frightened and disheartened young lady.

FOUR

There was a small bath adjoining the bedroom and I must admit Maggie was both competent and discreet. I felt not the slightest embarrassment as she attended my needs. After I was bathed, doing as much myself as possible, I napped. My travels had wearied me more completely than I thought. Also, the fact that I was now home didn't seem nearly as frightening as I'd expected it would. In fact, I felt comforted by it. It was as if the house embraced me. I suppose that sounds foolish—a domicile whose floors, walls and ceilings consisted of stone. Yet it was colorful and it reflected light beautifully and, to me, gave off a warmth. The place had been built by my grandfather and I know Papa and Mama felt a deep affection for it and took a modest pride in Bowen's Castle.

It was almost dark when I wakened. Maggie was seated by the side of the bed. She smiled and patted my hand.

"Feeling better?" she asked.

I was puzzled by her question. "If you mean rested—yes."

"Good. Would you like me to bring you a tray for supper, or will you eat with the family?"

"I'll dress and go to the dining room," I replied. "Did I dream, Maggie?"

She was already on her way to the closet. Apparently my bags had been unpacked while I slept.

"A little," she said. "You cried out three or four times."

I wasn't surprised. Many times in the hospital the nurses on the floor had been drawn to my room by my cries. They'd comforted me and urged me back to sleep, but the nightmare always left me spent. If only, I thought with an inward groan, it had been just a nightmare. But what I dreamt had actually happened.

She returned from the closet with a lovely pale green dinner gown.

"Where did you get that?" I exclaimed.

"It's your cousin's. She thought you might like to wear it tonight. It's a new style. Called Grecian."

I could see why. It was of soft chiffon and would drape beautifully on the body. It would show off the slender lines of my figure well, but it would also reveal my useless limbs and I preferred not to be reminded of them.

"That's kind of Cousin Rena," I said, "but I'll wear my pink taffeta tea gown. It has lace trim around the sleeves."

"I know the one," she said, reentering the closet. "We brought all your dresses downstairs this morning. Also, your undergarments. In this large closet there's plenty of room. There's a double chest in here too, for the overflow."

"I remember it," I said. I gripped the bedhead

and pulled myself to a sitting position. Maggie helped me dress, then wheeled me to the dressing table where I brushed my ash blond hair, piling it high and letting a few curls fall to my shoulders. I regarded my reflection in the mirror. I was very pale, but that was understandable. I'd get out of doors now and let the sun touch my skin to give it color. I had Mama's high cheekbones and blue eyes and Papa's stubborn chin and wide mouth. I remember once saying to her that I wished I had the beautifully-shaped lips she had, instead of my thin ones. She'd replied that Papa had given me his mouth because he wanted me to smile often and be happy. I'd felt content then. Now my thin-lipped, too-wide mouth seemed to mock me, for I felt I'd nothing to smile about.

I noticed Maggie's reflection. She was studying me and I sensed she was wondering the thought going through my mind. "You mustn't dwell on it," she said. "It's over and done with. I know. I kept wishing my Joseph alive again. It did no good."

"I can't help it, Maggie."

"Thinking about it is like poisoning yourself. Slow poison."

"Poison is too good for me," I said, lowering my gaze before her probing one.

"Finish your hair so I can take you in to supper. I'm to be allowed to eat at the table too."

"I should think so," I said. "I'd have it no other way."

I did smile then and this time it was she who looked away, but not before giving my shoulder a reassuring pat.

Dinner was pleasant. The dining room looked festive with vases of flowers placed about the room and a low centerpiece of blossoms on the table. The linen glowed with whiteness and the silver and crystal reflected the light from the myriad candles. That was one thing we had no fear of in a house of stone —fire. While items of furniture might burn through carelessness, the building would stand until eroded by time and that would take eons. There were over thirty rooms of all sizes and the edifice was three stories high.

The dinner was delicious; the talk, general. Aunt Liz asked if I would consent to allow her to plan a social of some kind. First of all, for the villagers to welcome me back; later, something more lavish, like a ball. It would be on a grand scale—like those Mama and Papa used to give. I asked her to please give me a week's time to become adjusted to my new way of living before committing myself. She agreed, but warned me she'd not let me bury myself alive in this fortress—as she called the house.

After dinner, Maggie wheeled me back to the den. Logs burned brightly in the large fireplace and I asked her to place me on the leather couch to one side of it, for the back was slanted upward and I could relax in the cheering warmth of the flames.

I then told Maggie she could have an hour to herself. "Where is your room?" I asked.

"It's on the third floor, Miss," she replied.

"That would hardly do me any good if I needed you through the night," I said.

"It would not, Miss. But Lorette said that's where I was to stay."

"This is one time my order will have to supercede

that of Lorette. For the time being, I would like you to sleep in here if you don't mind."

"It looks like a mighty comfortable couch, Miss," she said, eying it appreciatively. "If you don't mind, I'll go take a walk outside for a bit."

"I don't mind in the least," I replied. "I imagine the family will be in to visit me."

She was gone no more than a minute when Rena and Lew entered. I was puzzled by their somber features.

"Is something wrong?" I asked.

"We don't know," Lew said speculatively.

"What do you mean?"

"Well," Lew said, "I'm only your second cousin, which really doesn't make me very close."

"Please sit down, both of you," I said, suddenly aware of what was on their minds.

Lew chose a large leather chair. Rena settled herself on the stool at his feet.

Rena said, "I may as well ask right out. Now that you're back, do you wish us to leave?"

"Good gracious, no," I exclaimed. "I need you now more than ever."

"I don't think you do," Lew said, smiling. "You came back here fired with a zest for running the quarry."

I derided that. "I'm not going to run it. I'm just going to help. I must do something to keep my mind off myself. Just knowing you're both here warms my heart."

"Thank you, Betty," Lew said. "The thought of having to go out and work doesn't appeal to me. Now does the thought of having to live with my in-laws, as we did until the tragedy. They keep reminding me what a lazy lout their beautiful daughter married."

"She couldn't have found a more handsome husband," I said.

Rena smiled her appreciation. "Nor one with more charm."

"I agree," I said. "You're welcome to remain here for the rest of your lives if you wish."

"I do feel a pang of guilt though," Lew said. "After all, you're going to plunge yourself into work at the quarry, while I do nothing."

"If you won't object," I said, "I'll need someone to chauffeur me about. I'm going to make a trip to the village tomorrow to purchase some new frocks."

"Do let me come," Rena cried. "I'll help you make selections if you don't object."

"I have no objection," I said, smiling. "Your Grecian gown is beautiful. But I just didn't feel it was for me. Thanks though, for offering it."

Her face colored with embarrassment.

"What is it?" I asked.

"Your dressmaker Mrs. Adams made it for me. You'll get the bill."

"Fine," I said. "Make some more selections tomorrow."

Lew said, "I suppose I shouldn't bring this up, but I may as well tell you Aunt Liz and Uncle Elijah are concerned about whether or not you'll want them to remain, now that you've returned."

"Suppose you send them in so I can reassure them."

Lew came over to me, bent and kissed my brow. "I don't deserve you for a cousin. Thank you, Betty."

Rena blew me a kiss and they departed, followed

by the immediate entrance of Aunt Liz and Uncle Elijah. From the looks on their faces, I knew they sensed they'd not have to pack their bags and return to their modest flat in Boston. The four of them had come when tragedy struck and I'd asked them to remain when I was brought to the hospital so that the Castle would not be deserted. Since all four were in modest circumstances and I'd been blessed with wealth, I was not inclined to send them packing. The thought of being alone in the place—much as I loved it—repelled me.

I assured Aunt Liz and Uncle Elijah they were most welcome and I'd be unhappy if they left. Thus enheartened, they thanked me and, after a few more words of light chatter, they bade me good night and went upstairs to their room. Maggie came in shortly afterward, carrying her bed linen, nightdress, and wrapper. She picked me up, set me in the chair, then wheeled me into the bedroom. I was amazed at her strength and the ease with which she handled me. But I also resented it.

However, I knew I was blessed by her presence because everything went smoothly. She moved about quietly performing her chores. Observing her, I realized she was sturdily built, with not a trace of obesity on that large frame. She extinguished my lamp and retired to the den. I heard her quiet movements as she prepared herself for bed and I saw the light, reflected through the open door, go out.

Then all was quiet. It was an eerie sort of quiet, especially to one who was used to hearing hospital sounds. I'd completely forgotten the silence peculiar to a stone house. There was no creaking of boards. It was almost like being sealed in a tomb. I'd never had that thought before, but tonight I did and I felt a vague uneasiness.

I tried to think of the times it rang with the strains of light music and gay laughter. I even thought I could hear dim echoes of it, though the laughter now seemed derisive. I could see dancing figures whirling around and around while the laughter grew louder and louder until it became shrieks of hysteria, and I sat in their midst, terrified and helpless in my wheelchair. When I tried to escape, they closed in, arms extended, fingers pointing at me, their cachinnations growing ever more shrill and raucous. I covered my ears in an effort to shut it out, but to no avail.

Then someone was calling my name. I opened my eyes and blinked from the glow of the lamplight. It was Maggie, seated at my bedside.

"You had a nightmare," she said.

I could only nod, for I was still not free of the dreamworld filled with faces, grotesque in the degree of their distortion.

"Want to talk about it? Sometimes it helps."

"No."

"I'll sit by the bed 'til you go back to sleep." Her hand, holding mine, was reassuring.

"Please don't," I said. "I'll be all right."

"You're sure?"

"Quite."

She patted my hand, put out the lamp and returned to her bed in the den. I was bathed in perspiration and I was trembling, but I'd not allow myself to be babied. I was a coward. I knew it, but I'd make certain no one else did. I knew now that was my real reason for stating I was going to interest myself in the working of the quarry. I was afraid to live with myself. I feared thoughts filled with self-guilt. Nightmares that lingered long after I'd awakened.

It took me a long time, but I finally drifted off to sleep. It was bright daylight when I awakened. Maggie, ever-present, smiled a greeting.

"You slept late, but that's good. You look bright-eyed."

"I'm glad the day is pleasant. After breakfast, I'd like you to wheel me around the grounds. It's been a long time."

She looked dismayed. "You mean you want to go to the quarry, Miss?"

"Not today. I'm going to the village and select some new frocks. I'll ask Rena to come with me. Aunt Liz too if she wishes. So you'll have the afternoon to yourself."

"Thank you, Miss," she replied, in that serene way she had.

I had Maggie ring for Lorette and she brought a breakfast tray to my room. Aunt Liz came in to see how I was. She was ecstatic when I told her I intended a brief journey to the village for clothes and she was welcome to come along with Rena to make her selections as well. They'd be a gift from me and they were not to consider themselves obligated, as I needed their comforting presence.

For my inspection of the estate, I chose a simple blouse and skirt—a full one which would not call attention to my limbs. Maggie insisted I drape a light woolen shawl over my shoulders as the dew had been heavy and, despite the sun, there was dampness about. I did so and, with a light throw over my knees, we set out.

I'd forgotten some of the paths and so we found ourselves in a bottleneck now and then, from which we managed to extricate ourselves without too much trouble. A short distance beyond the house was a clearing with metal images of boys painted red and blue, implanted on white marble blocks. Each figure held a ring through which visitors might tie their mounts. There were some perennials in bloom, but a few more weeks would have to pass before the beds of varied flowers blossomed. I knew a gardener came each day for a few hours to prune and weed and mow the grass. I'd forgotten his name, but, in time, it would come to me. Even now, things that had slipped my mind were slowly coming back. Dr. Beardsley told me it was part of the trauma I'd suffered as a result of the accident. I still couldn't bear to think of the tragedy which had snuffed out the lives of my parents and for which I was completely responsible.

Maggie asked me if I wished to go back, but I refused. The freedom of the outdoors was stimulating and I found my spirits rising. I urged her to go on. We'd only gone a short distance when I cried out in fear.

"What is it?" she asked, my alarm seemingly transferred to her.

At first I couldn't answer, for my eyes were glued on the stark white marble tomb ahead of me. I'd never seen it before. I had no knowledge such a thing had been erected.

It was a massive building of fine marble, with an

iron gate, set in an arched entrance on which was carved the name Bowen. Above this, standing as if on guard over the door, was a life-sized angel, head bowed as if in sorrow, and robe held close to her body.

"When was that erected?" I gasped.

"After your mama and papa was killed, Miss," she said.

"I didn't think it was there before the accident. Who ordered it done?"

"Got no idea, Miss."

"Of course you wouldn't have. Please wheel me closer."

"Sure you want to see it, Miss?"

"Positive. And I will if the gate isn't locked."

"It ain't locked. I looked in there yesterday."

FIVE

She was right. There were three low steps to the entrance. She went up them and swung the iron-barred gate wide. She returned then and carefully maneuvered the chair up the steps and inside the tomb. I looked up at the sky and a rear view of the marble angel. Strange, I thought, the mausoleum hadn't been roofed.

The bodies of my grandparents had been exhumed and reinterred here, for their names were inscribed on the marble slabs covering two niches. The other two were engraved with the names of my parents. I glanced at the opposite side and stiffened in shocked horror, for one slab had already been carved. The name on it was mine. It bore the date of my birth. Following the word 'DIED' was a blank space.

My horror quickly changed to anger. "Who did that?"

"I don't know, Miss."

"Of course not. How could you? Please take me out of here."

"Will I bring you back to the house?"

"No. To the quarry."

"I'm not sure how to get there," she said.

"Retrace the path we took. It seems to me there's

one that branches off. As I recall, it's concealed by bushes which also conceal the stark walls of the quarry."

She followed my directions and, though we passed the partially concealed path, I soon realized it and had her go back. We found it and though there was a constant downward slope, it was gradual and provided no difficulty for Maggie in controlling the chair. But I was grateful, nonetheless, that she was so strong, for she'd have need of it when we made out ascent.

We finally reached the floor of the original quarry which had now been enlarged many times. This was where my grandfather discovered the practically endless supply of fine marble. The wooden shack where Reggie and Dudley worked was also the main office. There was even a faded sign over the door which read

BOWEN MARBLE WORKS

Dudley came out immediately, pencil over his ear, green shade peaked over his eyes and rolled up sleeves held in place by wide red elastic armbands.

"Morning, Miss Bess," he said. "Good to see you here. Want to come inside?"

"Not this morning, Dudley," I replied. "I just discovered the mausoleum. Who ordered it constructed?"

"Your papa did," Dudley said. "The plans for its design are in the office. Do you wish to see them?"

"No, thank you," I said. "I'm puzzled as to why I wasn't told about it."

"I expect because it was done right after the accident. You didn't talk to anyone for a long time after, Miss Betty. From what I hear, you just lay in your bed in the hospital, staring at the ceiling. You took it real hard, you know. It's understandable no one would mention the tomb."

"You're right, of course," I said. "It's beautiful."

"Especially the angel," he said.

"Yes," I admitted. "One gets a feeling of serenity just looking at it."

His mouth widened in a half smile. "Did it look familiar? The face, I mean."

"I didn't notice," I said. "Should it?"

"Well, sort of," he said evasively.

"Why was my name put on the slab?" I demanded.

"You'll have to ask Harley about that. He was in complete charge."

"Where is he?"

"At the house. He took a sample of that alomite for you to see."

"We'll go back then. But first I want to look over the quarry."

I asked Maggie to wheel me to the far side of it so I might observe the more recent cuts. Here, at the very bottom of the quarry, I felt insignificant. I always did, because the top was more than two hundred feet above, straight up along a solid wall still showing where the large blocks of marble had been extracted.

The machinery was making its usual din, though we were not so close to the channeling and cutting machines that we couldn't speak in normal tones.

"You seem to have progressed well," I said.

"Never did better," he said proudly. "We're cutting marble faster than ever and selling it before it's even broken free of the mountain. Keeps getting better in quality too. We've only begun to realize how valuable this quarry is."

"That's very good news," I replied. "We'll go back now, Maggie."

She turned the chair sharply and headed back for the path. I twisted around to wave Dudley a farewell. He smiled and waved back. Our ascent began immediately, but gradually Maggie slowed because pushing the chair and me uphill was no easy task, especially along a narrow dirt path that bordered the wall of the quarry. It was a perilous route and it would be fatal if she ever lost her hold of the chair. Fatal for me, because if the chair rolled backwards, I'd go over the side to sudden death.

Maggie was as relieved as I to get back on level ground. I insisted she pause for a few minutes to rest, for she was breathing rapidly from her exertions.

I recalled Dudley's question regarding the face of the angel. I wouldn't ask Maggie to wheel me all the way back to the tomb, yet I couldn't help wonder about it.

"Maggie, do you know what Dudley meant when he asked if the face of the angel looked familiar?"

"Yes, Miss," came the surprising reply.

I shifted around in my chair to look up at her. "Tell me, please."

"The angel has your face, Miss. I noticed it first thing today."

"Whoever did it certainly has a feeling for the macabre," I said sternly.

"I sort of think it was meant as a compliment to you," she replied, in that serene way she had of speaking.

"I'm not the least bit flattered by it," I said.

She made no reply. Nor did I pursue the topic further and we returned to the house in silence. I'd discuss it with Harley immediately. He undoubtedly had been in charge of the project, yet he must have consulted the family. I was annoyed that such a project had been undertaken while I was in no position to be consulted about it. I also was troubled with a feeling of apprehension regarding my name on the tombstone. That, to me, seemed premature and I'd certainly demand an explanation that would satisfy me.

Lorette opened the door for us and informed me Mr. Harley and Mr. Lew were in the den. I told Maggie she could use her room upstairs to rest, for I knew the climb had fatigued her. I continued on to the den, managing the chair quite expertly.

Harley and Lew arose at my entrance. Harley was holding a sizeable piece of marble which he offered to me. I studied it from every angle, then handed it back to him.

"So that's alomite," I said motioning the men to resume their seats.

Harley's voice warmed with enthusiasm. "I've never seen such perfect alomite. The dark blueness is beautiful, especially with the red veins and spots running through it."

"Have you any idea of how rich the vein is?"

"Not yet. We're going to start blasting tomorrow. It'll take a week longer before we know. However, I'll wager a guess that it goes quite far back. Maybe a thirty-or-forty-year supply."

"Splendid," I said, as pleased as he.

Lew said, "Harley said it makes the quarry worth three times as much as before."

"Of course I'm pleased," I said. "However, I'm just as displeased about a discovery I made while on a tour of the grounds."

Harley said, "Nothing's been changed. The only thing different is the tomb."

"The tomb," I repeated. "Dudley said it was Papa's idea."

"It was," Harley replied. "I'm surprised you didn't know about it."

"Neither Papa nor Mama ever mentioned it to me," I said.

"Perhaps they thought it too dismal a subject," Lew ventured.

"Perhaps," I said. "But, from the time I was fourteen, I was always included in discussions regarding not only the quarry, but the family and any plans they had in mind."

Harley's smile was apologetic. "I can't argue that point," he said. "I followed your father's orders."

"You mean you'd had discussions with Papa regarding the tomb?"

"At length and in great detail," Harley replied.

"Who else knew of it?" I asked.

"Perhaps no one other than Dudley and myself. I'm sorry you're upset about it, Betty. We couldn't consult with you, you know, and I felt—that is, Dudley and I—that since your papa had been going to erect a mausoleum, we should go ahead with it."

"Harley discussed it with us and asked our permission," Lew ventured.

I was still not mollified. "Was the angel atop it

part of Papa's plan? With my likeness on it?"

"That was Aunt Liz's idea," Lew said. "She felt there should be something erected to your memory."

"To my memory," I exclaimed in shocked dismay. "I didn't know I was so near death."

"You had no will to live," Lew said remindfully. "We received several letters from Dr. Beardsley stating there was no change in your condition and the greater amount of time that passed, the less chance there would be for your recovery."

"It was meant to honor you, Betty," Harley said. "After a consultation with the family, I suggested Raymond Stardis as the sculptor to do the angel. It's beautiful enough to grace any museum."

"I wish I knew one that would accept it," I said tartly. "I'm afraid I don't share your enthusiasm or that of the family as a way of remembering me."

"Do you wish me to have it removed?" Harley asked.

"No. However, I do want the stone covering the niche apparently reserved for me removed."

Harley arose. "It will be done immediately. I'm sorry, Betty. I'm sure none of us meant to hurt you."

I nodded understandingly, but asked, "Who ordered my name placed on that stone?"

"You weren't expected to get well," Lew replied, coloring uncomfortably.

I regarded both men. "I hope no one is disappointed I did."

Lew said, "That's a hell of a thing to say."

"I suppose it is," I replied. "And, despite your blasphemy, you still haven't answered my question."

"It was decided on at a meeting of the family," he said. "I can't remember who proposed it. In case it was I, I apologize."

"In case it was you, you should," I retorted. "And since the family was looking to the future, I don't know why you didn't assign yourselves a niche with your names carved on the slabs covering the openings. There's plenty of room for all of us."

"My God, Betty," don't be so bitter," Lew exclaimed.

Harley came over and regarded me apologetically. "I wish we'd waited until you returned, Betty. I'd give anything to undo the hurt you've been caused by it."

"I won't pretend I'm not hurt and dismiss it with a shrug. I was hurt and shocked and angry—all three at one time. I know my condition has, perhaps, made me oversensitive, but I feel, in this instance, if I have proven difficult, I should be forgiven."

"We're the ones to ask forgiveness," Harley said. "We erred. I admit it. Be assured, Betty, from now on, you'll be consulted before any order is accepted, or any shipment made."

I reached up and touched his arm reassuringly. "I'll get over it. I'm looking forward to our working together."

His smile was one of relief. "So am I. I'll have the slab with your name on it removed at once."

"Never mind, Harley," I said, returning the smile. "I agree with Lew. I am touchy. Let it stay for the time being. I don't wish to ride roughshod over you and the others. Just remember—I am the only surviving member of the Bowen family—meaning, I inherited the business. Please consult me on all future matters."

"You have my word on it," Harley said. "I must

get back now. Dudley and I are having a conference with some of the men regarding the dynamiting."

"Good," I approved. "It's time for my nap. I'm afraid my little expedition has left me spent."

Lew said, "Would you like me to send Maggie in?"

"She's resting," I said. "But if you'll just place me on the couch, I'm sure I'll be quite comfortable."

"Let me," Harley said, and before I could protest, I was in his arms and gently deposited on the couch. "Just remember, you've always been a very special young lady to me. And you'll continue to be."

"Thank you, Harley," I said, looking up at him. "I'm sure we'll enjoy working together. Just remember, I have great need of you."

He nodded his gratitude and I was surprised and mildly embarrassed to see his eyes soften as he regarded me. "That's good to hear. I'll not let you down again."

SIX

There was no need to inform the others of my displeasure regarding the tomb. Lew saw to it they were told and during supper that evening, Aunt Liz apologized, though stating she had my best interest at heart. I didn't quite know how to interpret it, but I accepted her statement, certain it was made in good faith.

The next four days passed quickly. Twice, during that time, Aunt Liz, Rena and I paid Mrs. Adams, the village dressmaker, a visit. I made several selections, both of dresses and negligees for, confined to my chair as I was, I had a goodly need of the latter. Though she was quite a reserved woman, she was clever with the needle and also very astute. For she selected gowns with panels and ruffles beginning at the waistline in the front and extending to the hem. Aunt Liz fussed, saying I was being overly sensitive —which I was—and all those frills would conceal my shapely form. She was undoubtedly right, but it was what I wanted. Most of all, the designs served to hide my useless limbs.

Harley, true to his word, came each afternoon and discussed the progress they had made or would endeavor to make the following day. He was most enthusiastic about the vein of alomite, certain now that it was extensive. They had already dynamited that section, but more blasting was necessary.

By the fifth day I felt completely rested and, much to my surprise, there were times when I even forgot I was confined to a wheelchair. The thought pleased me to a certain extent though I resented it too because I didn't ever want to forget my handicap, nor the reason for it. That was my punishment for carelessness.

It was mid-afternoon when Maggie wheeled me outside. Dudley had come with the books and had spent the morning and part of the afternoon explaining them to me. They were beautifully kept and he was quite zealous as he pointed out balances, all in the profit column. I was most pleased.

Of course, I knew I was a wealthy young lady, for Mr. Parnell, president of the bank and trustee for the estate, had paid me a visit yesterday. He, too, went into detail as to my worth. When I told him I wished my aunt and uncle and my cousins to receive an allowance each week, he nodded obediently, though he tugged at his Vandyke beard thoughtfully. I had the feeling he didn't approve, but since it was what I wanted, I didn't question his silence.

Maggie asked me if there was any particular part of the estate I wished to see. When I said there wasn't, she suggested the area bordering the quarry. I hesitated, but only for a moment. It was the place where Mama and Papa had met their tragic end.

"I suppose you may as well take me there," I said, though inwardly reluctant about going. "I can't avoid the spot the rest of my ilfe."

"That's for sure, Miss," she said. "You have to face it. It's over."

"It will never be over for me, Maggie," I said.

"Time heals everything, Miss. I know. I thought I'd never get over my Joseph."

"You had nothing to do with your husband's death," I said.

"True," she admitted. "I suppose it makes a difference."

"A very great one. Nonetheless, take me there."

She glanced at her lapel watch. "I believe there's time. That is, if you're not too tired. You shouldn't have let that Dudley Seaver stay so long."

"I had no idea of the time," I said. "Besides, I think he enjoyed having a hot dinner with the family, instead of a cold sandwich from a lunch pail."

"He ate his fill, that's for sure," she said. "You're good to your help, Miss. But then, so was your papa. He fired my Joseph more times than I can remember, then took him back."

"I wish Papa hadn't re-hired him. Your Joseph might be alive today."

"I agree. But we can't change what's happened."

"I know. It's one of the tragedies of life."

"Are you a coward, Miss?"

Despite the soft-spoken question, I was stunned, for it came so unexpectedly. "Of course not."

"Then you shouldn't be afraid to see where the accident happened."

"Just don't go too close to the edge," I said, suddenly aware that my morning's concentration on the books had wearied me. "In fact, I believe I've had . . ."

I never did finish the sentence, for the earth shook beneath us and sod, stones and dirt shot skyward from a dynamite explosion. The wall of the quarry was about a hundred yards ahead of us. The explosion had been in that area and near the top of the wall.

The ground sloped downward which was why I'd asked her to be cautious about going too near the edge. At the moment of the explosion, Maggie, whose voice I'd never heard raised, screamed and, in her fear, released her hold on the wheelchair. It began to roll and my screams were added to hers. I didn't know if she'd recovered her senses sufficiently to pursue me. I was too busy attempting to stop the chair, but it had gained too much momentum. Despite my frantic efforts, all I did was burn the skin of both palms as the wheels spun madly beneath them.

The chair, slanted downward, was bringing me closer and closer to the edge of the quarry. If it went over, I'd be killed. I didn't even stop to think it was what I'd been wanting since the tragedy. I made another attempt to stop the chair or, at least, change its course, but to no avail. Now I heard Maggie's screeches for help and she sounded closer, but I couldn't risk looking behind me. I heaved my weight from side to side to try and tilt the chair. It was no use. My efforts accomplished nothing and I kept going at a speed that, in no way, lessened.

I was not more than ten feet from the edge of the quarry now and heading in a direction that would take me overside. I'd just about given up hope when I felt a jar and the chair slowed a trifle. Maggie had managed to reach me. She gave the chair a hard wrench, pulling it back. The momentum threw me to the ground. I fell heavily, helpless to stop my rolling and sliding, but I'd managed to twist my body so I rolled parallel to the edge, rather than heading for it.

I was screaming when Maggie caught up with me again. This time she grasped one wrist and held on so that I was jerked to a stop. She dropped down beside me, too winded to speak, still too terrified to even think, I suppose, because that was how I felt.

"Couldn't . . . stop the thing," she finally managed. "Never knew . . . I could run that fast. My fault . . ."

"Don't apologize. You saved my life."

"My fault," she grumbled. Then she looked at me sharply. "You hurt, Miss? Been cut some and there's blood. Any bones broken?"

"I don't think so," I said.

"Bones busted you wouldn't have to wonder," she said.

"There's no feeling in my legs, Maggie. They could be broken a dozen times and I'd not know it."

"Got to get you back to the house and fetch a doctor," she said. "Don't move. I'll get the chair."

She retrieved it, got me into it and even before she tucked the blanket around me, I realized I did, indeed, need a physician. I ached in every bone above my waist and my hands became bloodstained when I passed them over my face. By the time we reached the house, besides being shaken, I was dizzy and faint.

Lorette exclaimed in dismay when she saw me and led the way to my bedroom. Maggie transferred me to the bed, while Lorette went into the bath for a basin of water, washcloth and towels. She set them on the table beside the bed and was about to help undress me, but I told her to find Lew and send him to the village for the doctor.

"Right away, Miss Betty," she said, hastening from the room.

I heard her call Lew and his quick response. He didn't even come in and I was glad, for it was a good ride to the village and I felt as if my entire insides had been torn loose. I'd fallen with such force the breath had been knocked out of me. I lay there, completely spent, while Maggie ministered to me.

Her hands were skilled and gentle and she bathed the dirt from my face and hands. The latter had been burned from the wheels spinning against them. Aunt Liz and Rena came in and assisted by bringing basins of clean water. They worked in silence, their anxiety evident in their faces.

I thanked them and they left the room. Maggie helped me remove the remainder of my garments and get into my nightdress.

"You have to rest now," she said. "That was a terrible thing."

Aunt Liz stuck her head in the door. "Is there something we can do for you, dear?"

"Nothing, thank you," I replied.

"Just what happened?" she asked.

"There was a dynamite explosion," I said. "We became frightened."

"I'm to blame, Mrs. Pauley," Maggie said. "I was so stunned, I let go of the chair. We were on the grounds near the quarry wall."

"Oh, good heavens," Aunt Liz exclaimed. "You could have gone over."

"She almost did," Maggie said. "But she had enough

sense to twist her body and roll in another direction."

"Why did you ever go there, child?" Aunt Liz asked.

"I don't really know," I said. And I didn't. I suppose it was a sudden impulse.

We heard the doorbell. Then the door opened and male voices were evident.

Aunt Liz's head disappeared for a moment, then reappeared. "It's Harley and Dudley. They heard the screams and came at once."

"Let them come in," I said. "Please put another pillow under me, Maggie."

She did, using the utmost care, but even so I cried out, for the slightest movement sent pain shooting through my body. I ached from head to foot. My hands burned so, it seemed as if I were holding live coals.

Harley, Dudley and Uncle Elijah entered, all looking concerned.

"I'm quite all right," I said, managing a reassuring smile.

"My God, I hope so," Harley said. "What were you doing near the quarry? You knew we were blasting."

"It was a sudden whim," I said.

"No more whims until the blasting is over," he said, softening his words with a smile. "Promise?"

"I promise," I said. "It was stupid of me now that I think of it."

"No," he contradicted. "We should send word up here whenever we're going to blast. But since—since you went to the hospital, no one ever goes near the grounds that edge the wall of the quarry."

"Indeed, we don't," Uncle Elijah asserted. "We don't want a repetition of the accident."

I closed my eyes, for I was suddenly back there, reliving that awful day.

"I'm sorry, my dear," Uncle Elijah said apologetically. "That was a tactless remark."

I looked up at him. "I know you meant nothing by it. I wish I could stop this wretched despondency that overwhelms me whenever I think of that horrible day."

Dudley addressed Harley. 'Don't you think we should send word to the Castle whenever we're going to dynamite from now on?"

"We will." Harley spoke with quiet firmness.

"It won't be necessary," I said. "I shan't go near there again."

"Not for awhile anyway," Maggie said. "Now if you'll all please go out. Miss Betty needs rest and quiet. Dr. Egan's been sent for and he'll see if there's any more than cuts and bruises."

They filed out obediently. Maggie closed the door after them. "Close your eyes and rest, Miss. I'll sit over by the window."

"Thank you, Maggie, for being so competent."

"It's what I'm paid for, Miss. Just sorry you had to go through such a thing. Terrible memories all brought back. Don't think about it."

I didn't want to, but it seemed that it was on everyone's mind and, in their concern, they couldn't help but refer to it. I closed my eyes and rested, relieved that Maggie had presence of mind enough to send everyone from the room. Talking had been an effort. Even thinking. I don't know how long I lay there before Dr. Egan arrived, but I was beginning to feel a little better.

Aunt Liz tapped on the door and called that the doctor had arrived. Maggie let him in.

I'd expected an older man, but Dr. Jeffrey Egan, as he introduced himself, was young. However, he had an assured manner that commanded immediate confidence and respect. He placed his hat on the table and walked over to the bedside, carrying his black bag.

"Hello, Mrs. Morfit. At least I know my patient is in good hands. Tell me what happened."

Since he addressed Maggie, I lay quietly while she related, in detail, our misadvanture and the cause of it. It gave me an opportunity to observe him more closely. He was clean shaven, which I liked, with dark brown eyes that were quietly observant. He took out his watch and checked my pulse. At the same time he was regarding my bruised face. Next, he examined the palms of my hands.

"I'll bandage your hands so they'll be protected. Fortunately, the burns are superficial, so after a few days, the pain will ease."

"Thank you, doctor," I said.

He took bandage from his bag and went to work. Late afternoon sunlight touched his auburn hair, deepening its color. There was a slight unruliness to it which I imagine he found annoying, but which gave him a boyish air.

"I'm pleased you came so promptly," I said. "But I'm surprised. I expected Dr. Reed."

"He died while you were away. I've taken his place." He spoke while continuing his work, now moving around to the other side of the bed to bandage my right hand. "Do you have sharp pains in any part of your body?"

"No. I'm just sore all over. I guess I panicked at first, mostly because of my legs, I guess."

"I'll examine them, along with the rest of you just to make certain nothing's broken."

Maggie stood at the foot of the bed while he subjected me to a rigorous examination, satisfying himself that I was really not injured beyond the scrapes and bruises which he now proceeded to attend to.

When he finished, he said, "You were fortunate. Falling out of a wheelchair can be a serious thing for someone with your disability."

"I know," I said.

He drew up a chair beside the bed. "Mrs. Morfit, you may be excused. I want to talk with Miss Bowen and get some first hand information regarding her injury."

"Please go upstairs and lie down, Maggie," I said. "You must be exhausted."

"I'm all right, Miss," she assured me. "But I'll rest until Doctor leaves. Just have Lorette call me."

"If she doesn't, I will," Dr. Egan said. His voice was resonant and I liked the sound of it.

Maggie left us, closing the door behind her. "Your cousin, Mr. Lew Hutching, informed me you'd been in the hospital for two years. Will you tell me about it?"

"Rutland, at first. When they couldn't help me, they suggested Boston General."

"And you met with no more success there?"

"None."

"Were you in Dr. Beardsley's care?"

"Yes. Do you know him?"

Dr. Egan smiled. "I trained under him. He's one of the best in the profession. What did he tell you about your condition?"

"He didn't have to tell me anything. I know I'll never walk again."

Dr. Egan looked his surprise. "You didn't answer my question, Miss Bowen."

"I think I did."

He eyed me with disapproval. "You did not."

"I don't like your tone of voice, Doctor. You came here to see whether or not I might have a serious injury as a result of my fall from the wheelchair. I haven't. If you'll tell me what your fee is, I'll write you a check."

"No need to. I'll mail you a bill." He arose, snapped his bag shut and looked down at me. "If you have any further problems, send for me. Otherwise, I shan't bother you."

"Nor shall I bother you," I said. "I'm sorry I inconvenienced you."

"No inconvenience, Miss Bowen. The only thing is, when I first looked at you, I thought you were a well-adjusted young lady. I rather pride myself on being a conscientious doctor and I can usually judge the type of patient a person will be when I enter a room. I'm far more annoyed with myself that I was so wrong about you."

I was astounded at his boldness. I tried to sit up, but cried out with pain and fell back on my pillows, as my muscles protested. He made no effort to console me.

"What are you talking about?" I blurted.

"That you're so consumed with self-pity, you're

actually childish."

"That's ridiculous," I exclaimed.

"It's the truth and you know it."

"Please leave, Doctor. At once."

"I shall." He picked up his hat and bowed his head slightly. I couldn't tell if the gesture was one of mockery because my eyes were blurred with tears. I turned my head so he wouldn't see them. I heard the door open and close, followed by the sound of muted voices which drifted through. A moment later, Aunt Liz entered, followed by Rena.

Rena said, "My, my, what a handsome doctor. I wish I'd been the one to have fallen out of the wheelchair."

I managed to keep my voice calm as I said, "He's so rude he's detestable."

"Good gracious," Aunt Liz exclaimed. "He didn't say that about you."

"No, he didn't," Rena said coyly. "He told us that if you had very much pain to send for him. He also left a sleeping draught for you to take and assure you of a good night's rest."

"I'll have no need of it," I said.

Aunt Liz said, "He also told us you were very brave. And don't look so cynical. He did say that, didn't he, Rena?"

"Yes," she replied.

"He's visited the quarry a few times," Aunt Liz went on. "He told Lew the first time was to attend an employee who was injured there. He found it such a fascinating place he goes there whenever he finds time."

"So long as he doesn't get in the way of the workers, I doubt anyone will object. Now, if you don't mind, I'd like to rest. I'm very tired."

"You should be," Aunt Liz consoled. "That was a horrible thing. I'm wondering if we should dismiss Maggie for carelessness."

"No," I exclaimed. "I was as terrified as she. She didn't mean to let go of the wheelchair. And if she hadn't run and got hold of it . . ."

"Spilling you out in the process," Rena broke in.

"Her doing so probably saved my life," I said.

"No matter how frightened she got," Aunt Liz said, "she shouldn't have let go. You're helpless by yourself."

"As if I didn't know," I said. "Well, it's over now and I'm still here, so we won't hold it against Maggie. She's extremely competent and you know it."

"I suppose she is," Aunt Liz said, though not sounding convinced.

"And if she left, do you think either of you would be able to lift me, help me dress and bathe?"

"There's Lorette," Rena suggested.

"She has the responsibility of the Castle. And she's just one person. Maggie stays," I said. "We'll have no further discussion of it."

Aunt Liz touched my bruised shoulder in an affectionate gesture. It was all I could do to keep from crying out, but I managed, for I didn't wish to upset her. "Rest, my dear. We'll have supper sent in to you."

"A light collation, please. I really have no appetite."

"Nonetheless, you need nourishment to give you strength."

"Very well, Aunt Liz."

I closed my eyes. I was spent and had no further

desire to converse. They left quietly. The sound of the door closing was pleasant to hear. I wanted to cry, for I felt so very alone. I was hurt by Dr. Egan's gruff manner. Hurt and deeply offended. I had no further desire to see him and I knew that if I ever needed a doctor, I'd go to Rutland rather than submit to his arrogance.

Fortunately, I managed to drift off. I awakened to lamplight, with Maggie sitting at my bedside.

"Feeling better?" she asked.

"A little," I replied.

"I'll bring you some soup. You don't want any more than that."

I nodded briefly and let her spoon feed it to me for, with both hands bandaged, I knew I couldn't manage it myself.

She wouldn't let the others in again and I was relieved. She insisted though, I take the sleeping draught, stating what my body needed was rest and relaxation and I'd not get it without help. I didn't argue, for I seemed sorer than ever and the slightest movement made me wince.

SEVEN

A week passed and with each day the pain lessened. I refused to allow Maggie to bandage my hands, for I no longer felt pain and the rawness was already fading as the skin began to renew itself.

Lorette brought me in the mail each day. It consisted mostly of household bills which I sent on to Mr. Parnell at the bank. He could take care of them until I was able to write again. Along with it was a bill from Dr. Egan. Much to my surprise, a note was included. At first, I was tempted to toss it into the fireplace, unread, but, in true feminine fashion, my curiosity got the better of me. It began:

Dear Miss Bowen:

I hope, by now, your bruises and pain have abated to the extent that you are able to resume your daily activities. I also apologize for having offended you.

As I told you, my annoyance was directed toward myself since I erred in believing you to be a well-adjusted young lady, rather than one consumed with self-pity. But I'm certain the eminent Dr. Beardsley told you that, though I doubt you'd ever admit it.

I hope you won't consider my fee exorbitant for my services. I'll be frank to admit I've rendered a substantial bill. And the reason—to help pay for medications for patients unable to buy them.

Sincerely,
Jeffrey Egan, M.D.

My face flamed with anger and I wheeled my chair over to the fireplace to toss the impudent letter into the flames. On second thought, I kept it. I don't know why, except that I felt to reread it would increase my dislike of the arrogant doctor.

I had Maggie take me out for some air, but I was no sooner out than I asked her to bring me back. I consented when she asked if she might take the buggy and go to the village. The rest from her chores would do her good. I summoned Aunt Liz and Rena and suggested a drive. They were willing, but Lew had already gone into the village with the carriage on an errand. I knew we had a second and asked why Uncle Elijah couldn't handle the reins. Aunt Liz informed me he was having a very severe attack of gout. She seemed highly nervous. So was I. Dr. Egan's letter had upset me deeply.

What upset me even more was the sight of a buggy moving down the drive. The gentleman holding the reins was Dr. Egan. I moved my chair away from the window and headed for the hall. If he'd come to apologize for the letter he'd written, I'd send him on his way quickly. Such insolence was inexcusable.

Both Lorette and Aunt Liz were standing in the now-open doorway. They turned and regarded me apprehensively. Though I'd made no mention of the disfavor in which I held the doctor, they had sensed my disapproval of him and his name had not been brought into any conversation since the day he paid me a professional visit.

"You may go about your business," I told them, moving imperiously to the door. "I'll attend to the doctor. I have no need of him."

"Please, dear," Aunt Liz extended a hand in a beseeching gesture. "I sent Lew in to ask Doctor to come here for Elijah. He has a great deal of pain in his toe and ankle."

"I didn't know Uncle Elijah was troubled with gout."

"As we get older," she said quietly, "we become afflicted with the illnesses common to our age."

"You should have told me you'd summoned Dr. Egan."

"We were afraid you'd forbid his coming here," she said, smiling apologetically.

I made an impatient gesture with my hand. "Oh, come now, Aunt Liz, I'm not an ogre."

"Of course you're not, dear. But we sensed the doctor had offended you in some manner."

"Not professionally," I replied. "When he's finished with Uncle Elijah, tell him I wish to see him."

Aunt Liz's smile was one of relief. "I'm so glad. I'm sure he will do everything he can to help you."

Even Lorette's face brightened. "May I wheel you back to the den, Miss Betty?"

"Yes, and quickly—before he comes in."

I had no intention of forgiving him. I merely wished to give him a check which I would write out while he was upstairs. I'd tried using a pen this morning and found I could manage it without too much difficulty. I had Lorette wheel me to the desk, then I dismissed her.

I took out the checkbook and wrote an amount double the fee on the bill I'd received. I wasn't unappreciative of the good work Dr. Egan was doing in the village and this would be proof of it.

About twenty minutes passed before Lorette escorted him to the den. She closed the door quietly behind her. He paused just inside the door, his demeanor polite, but formal, yet I sensed his eyes regarding me in a professional manner.

I extended the check. "I received your bill this morning. Here is the payment."

He walked over and took it, glancing briefly at it. "There's no need for you to be so generous."

"I don't consider it in that manner. I'm pleased you're taking a personal interest in the poor of the village."

"Every decent doctor does what I'm doing," he replied. "They prefer keeping quiet about it."

"I have no intention of mentioning it to anyone. I just wished you to know I approved."

He held up the check. "It's twice the amount I billed you. Is that meant to impress me?"

I stiffened with anger. "Certainly not."

He smiled. "I'm glad, because I don't impress easily."

I said, "Bad manners, in which you seem to excel, have never impressed me." I hoped the contempt in my eyes matched that of my voice.

"I'd apologize except that I doubt you're as angry with me as you are with the letter I wrote."

I took a deep breath and exhaled slowly before replying. "Yes, your letter did make me angry."

"I'm glad because, once your anger abates, you might start some constructive thinking and you'll know every word in that letter, referring to your condition, is the truth."

"It is not," I said.

He slipped the check into his pocket. "I'm afraid you'll have to excuse me. I'm too busy to waste more time bandying words."

"I apologize for taking up your time," I said.

He regarded my hands, lying palms upward in my lap. "I trust the burns on your hands are healing."

"Beautifully," I said. "And the bruises and bumps have subsided. I'm in excellent health, Doctor, fortunately for me."

"With the exception of your legs, I'd say you were an excellent specimen of womanhood. Physically, that is. Mentally, you're very crippled. Good day, Miss Bowen."

"Dr. Egan," I exclaimed. "How dare you!"

He walked over to me, slowly but so determinedly I backed my chair until it struck the desk. He paused only inches away from me.

"I dare because I am not beholden to you," he said quietly.

"No one is beholden to me," I retorted.

"Two middle-aged people upstairs are," he replied. "Oh, I know you've treated them courteously. Even allowing them to live here during your sojourn in the hospital when you took up bed space without endeavoring in the least to cooperate."

"That's a lie."

"It's the truth. As for your kindness to your aunt and uncle, I'm not impressed. They told me your father sent them a generous check regularly. I think they'd be happier back in their apartment in Boston. At least, they wouldn't have to be fearful of offending you—especially when they have need of medical care and are quite aware you loathe my presence in this house."

"I cannot believe my aunt and uncle made that statement."

"They made no such statement. But before I came down, your aunt pleaded with me not to antagonize you."

"If they're so unhappy here, why don't they return to Boston? I'll inform them they'll have no financial worries there."

"Do you really want to know why they're remaining here?"

I met his gaze boldly. "Yes."

"They don't wish to leave you alone. They're greatly concerned about you."

"There is no need for them to be," I replied. "I'll inform them they're welcome to stay or go as they wish."

His brows raised thoughtfully. "I was hoping you wouldn't be so unkind. I didn't want them to know I mentioned their fears of offending you."

"Be assured I'll be tactful," I said primly.

"I doubt it," he said.

"There is no further need for us to bandy words, to use your phrase. In your eyes, I could make no kind gesture. To you, I'm the wealthy heiress whose subjects must pay homage."

He smiled. "Are you, Miss Bowen? It seems as if I did recall Maggie referring to you as the Princess."

"So I heard, though I'd forgotten. So long as she doesn't use the term in my presence, I don't mind how she thinks of me."

"I'm sure she thinks it in a complimentary sense."

I held back a sigh of despair. I was weary of verbal duels. "Dr. Egan, so long as my uncle needs your skill, please attend to his needs."

"Thank you, Miss Bowen. I would like to look in on him tomorrow."

"By all means, do so. Just remember, you don't need my permission to come here to treat any occupant in the house."

"Thank you," he said, again with that slight bow of his head.

"Nor do you need to thank me," I said. "Good day, Doctor."

"Do you wish the door closed?" he asked.

"Yes, please," I said.

He did so, quietly, and I wheeled the chair over to the window to watch him depart. He untethered the animal from the low post which stood just beyond the porch and was about to get in the buggy when he turned. It was almost as if he sensed I was regarding him. I couldn't move the chair fast enough to elude his gaze. A smile touched his mouth and his hand raised in a farewell wave. I didn't return it. I was certain he didn't expect me to. He knew, discerning as he was, I was embarrassed that he'd seen me. I wondered if he also knew he'd reached the inner recesses of my mind. That he'd succeeded in making me feel ashamed of myself. That I knew, finally, I had been indulging in self-pity, just as Dr. Beardsley had said.

I moved away from the window and rang for Lorette. I asked her to tell Aunt Liz I'd like to see her whenever it was convenient for her to come.

Aunt Liz came immediately. She was breathless from her exertions. "I hope I didn't keep you waiting, my dear."

"I didn't mean for you to rush, Aunt Liz," I said.

"Your uncle is resting. Doctor says he has to remain in bed for a few days."

"Dr. Egan said he'd keep a close check on Uncle Elijah," I replied.

Her smile was apologetic. "Your uncle thinks highly of the doctor, if you don't mind my saying so."

"So do I," I told her, hoping my smile was reassuring. "And when he comes tomorrow—which he told me he would do—will you tell him, please, I would like to see him?"

"Of course, my dear," she said. She regarded me speculatively, as if uncertain whether to voice the thought which was in her mind. "You know, for the first time since you came home, you seem like the girl who made these halls ring with gay laughter. You have your father's gift in that respect, though your mama was also a happy person to be around. I hope you don't mind my mentioning them."

"No," I said, and found I didn't. "I'm afraid I made a bad mistake in not talking about them. I think about them constantly."

I saw her glance shift to my legs and, as quickly, look away. "You had a terrible shock. More so, since you were on the verge of womanhood when it happened. I won't dwell on it, Betty, because I know how painful it is to you. But your mind must adjust because you do have a life ahead of you and you mustn't spend it wrapped up in the quarry. You have competent men to do that."

"Yes," I admitted. "But just as soon as my bruises heal, I'm going to be a part of that business. I like it and I know Papa wanted it that way."

"Yes, he did," she admitted. "He said you had the mind for it."

I smiled again. "I shan't let him down."

Concern etched her features. "My dear, please stay away from the quarry."

"Aunt Liz," I said firmly, "I must stop being afraid. I've been afraid to think, yet I never stopped thinking. I've been afraid to talk of Mama and Papa, yet they've been constantly in my mind. I was afraid of the quarry. What happened a week ago didn't help, but I survived it. Now I must clear my mind of all fear."

"I suppose you're right," she said dubiously. "In any event, I'll tell Elijah you're not mad at the nice Dr. Egan."

I couldn't help but laugh. "Tell Uncle Elijah also I hope he gets well soon."

"Doctor said it would help if he was a little more cautious about his diet. I told Lorette and she's going to see to it he gets nothing except what he's supposed to."

"He'll probably be very unhappy," I said.

"He will indeed," she agreed. "But he was getting a little too heavy. However, he is annoyed he can't groom and care for the horses. He's done it ever since you were away, you know."

"I didn't know. I didn't even think about it. But there's no need for that. We can hire a stableman."

"Don't do it," she said. "Let Lew take charge now. Elijah told him this morning he'd have to. He might as well do something to earn his keep."

"I don't expect him to, Aunt Liz."

"Don't spoil him any more than he is now, Betty. Both he and Rena are very lazy. A pity they don't have wealth so they could indulge themselves with parties and travels. Don't forget, I expect you to let me know when you're ready to resume social activities. That's something I know about."

"Thank you, Aunt Liz. I will."

The next day after Dr. Egan had looked in on Uncle Elijah, he came to the den. He immediately excused Maggie, set his bag on a table and drew up a chair to face the one I occupied.

He took my hands in his and examined the palms. "They're healing beautifully. I hope the rest of you is going as well."

"It is, Doctor," I said. "I had a definite reason for asking you to see me."

He smiled. "You're not angry any more."

"True. I came to my senses."

"Good. I was rough on you."

"I deserved it."

"You needed to be jolted out of that negative state of mind you'd cultivated. Just what is it you wish of me?"

"Perhaps too much," I replied soberly. "But I'm willing to place myself in your care."

He regarded me cautiously, as if not quite believing. "You want me to try and help you regain the use of your legs."

"Yes."

"And you're willing?"

"Very," I assured him.

"Suppose I take you out for a stroll. The first thing you have to do is tell me about the accident.

We'll find a tranquil spot where we can talk."

"You may leave your bag here, Doctor."

"Oh no," came his swift reply. "This is a professional visit."

I directed him to an area secluded on three sides by pine trees in front of which were marble benches. He set his hat and bag on the bench and dropped onto the ground to face me.

He smiled. "Suppose we start anew."

"A good idea. Just where shall we begin?"

"With the accident. I want to know all you remember about it."

I sobered quickly. "I don't know if I can talk about it."

"You must. You have to completely rid yourself of that mental block. First of all, did your parents love you?"

"Very much. That's what makes it so unendurable."

"Didn't you love them?"

"Of course," I said sharply.

He raised a restraining hand. "Don't get angry. I know you're obsessed with a feeling of guilt and I must find the reason for it. Therefore, from time to time, I'll ask questions which will irritate you, but try to be patient with me. I must ask them and you must answer, as completely and honestly as possible."

"Very well, Doctor. My life with my parents was beautiful. They were never embarrassed to display affection for each other in my presence. And they gave me generously of their love."

"Which you returned."

"With all my heart."

"Then why are you feeling guilty?"

"Because it was my carelessness that caused the dynamite explosion that killed them."

"How can you be so certain?"

"Though for a time I suffered a loss of memory, I now completely recall everything. I could show you exactly what happened."

"Suppose we go there." He was on his feet before I could protest. "Don't tell me that was where you had the accident the other day. I know it was. I had your cousin Lew bring me there."

"You mean you came back here without my being aware of it?"

He chuckled. "Two or three times."

"Then if you know about the accident which killed my parents, why must we go there?"

"I want to take you there so you can point out the places where your parents were standing. Also, where the wire and battery box were located."

While he talked, he'd turned the chair around and headed in the direction of the quarry wall. I couldn't hold onto the chair arms tightly, for my hands were still sore and the skin had not nearly replenished itself. But I tensed, for I wondered if I could endure going back there. And when we came in sight of it, I closed my eyes, for my sudden anguish seemed unbearable.

Apparently Dr. Egan sensed my emotional upheaval, for his hand lightly touched my shoulder. Only for a few moments, but it served to quiet my apprehension and relax me.

"Is this too close to the quarry wall for you?" he asked.

"No," I said. Then, daringly, added, "You may

wheel me along the edge of it if you wish."

"Not today," he said. "But I'm glad to hear you say that. It proves you can overcome your mental problem."

"What about my legs?"

"Before we discuss that, I want to hear about the accident." He stopped the chair at an angle so I had a sweeping view of the area where the tragedy occurred. He made certain the chair was secured by a large rock and as if to insure the fact I'd not have a repetition of what had happened a week ago, he sat on the ground in front of me.

"It happened a little over two years ago, on my parents' eighteenth wedding anniversary. They wished to celebrate it quietly, along with me. The following Saturday they intended to have a ball at the Castle, but this day they wished to be private and special. I felt so honored to be included in the celebration, though I don't know why I should think it anything special because they always included me. Yet I did. Mama had ordered a beautiful frock for me. It was my first taffeta gown—a pale blue with rows of tiny pink bows around the deep hem of the skirt. I attended school in Rutland, but was allowed to come home for the occasion. Mama and Papa met me at the depot. She was already dressed in a lovely lavender gown and when we arrived at the Castle, she sent me upstairs to change. They were going to take a walk along the grounds and told me they would meet me at this area where we are now. They walked here every day when weather permitted and very close to the cliff, for Papa liked to look down and point out to Mama and me the progress of the quarry. It's dug floor by floor, as you probably know."

"I know very little," Dr. Egan said. "I've been there a few times, but merely to observe. Harley and Dudley never waste a moment."

"Indeed not. They're very dedicated. Papa knew that and felt most fortunate in having them, not only because of their diligence, but because of their knowledge of marble and how to quarry it."

"You'd gone upstairs to change to your lovely new dress," Dr. Egan prompted.

"Yes," I replied. "I was in an ecstasy over it. And because I was impatient to express my appreciation, I ran madly across the grounds to where they were. When I came in view of them, I called out my delight with the dress and blew kisses with both hands. Their arms extended to me and I lifted my skirts to run faster, without looking at the ground. I wanted only to reach my parents, to embrace them and to be close to their love. But I never did." My hands covered my mouth as if to hold back a sob.

Dr. Egan reached up and gently drew my hands down. "Go on, Betty. I know it hurts, but you must tell it."

It wasn't until later I realized he'd addressed me informally. "My foot caught on a wire I didn't know was there. It was linked to a battery plunger used to set off dynamite. The sticks were already in place, almost directly below where Papa and Mama stood. The battery box was on the ledge, but the grass was high in that spot and it wouldn't be seen. When my foot encountered the wire, the box fell over the edge of the cliff. It hit the quarry wall in such a manner that the plunger was forced all the way down and contact was made. The dynamite blew up. My parents were killed. I was knocked down by the blast and a large rock thrown into the air by the explosion landed on my legs. It took an hour before they were able to remove the boulder. Though I blacked out, I believe I regained consciousness shortly after the blast, so I knew what had happened to Mama and Papa. I wanted to die. I just wanted to die. I kept saying it over and over and the months I spent in the hospital I again said it over and over and over. It became my credo."

"Your grief is understandable," Dr. Egan said. "Tell me, a week ago when you and Maggie were caught here by the dynamite explosion and, in her fright, she released her hold on the chair, did you want to die then?"

I thought back. "I don't know."

"Did you try to stop yourself?" he asked.

"Oh yes. I did everything I could think of. Trying to break the wheels with my hands, trying to tilt the chair so it would topple on its side. I was terrified."

"Did you want to go over the wall of the quarry and plunge to certain death?" he prompted.

"No," I said, with sudden awareness. "No, I didn't. When Maggie grabbed the chair and halted its descent, I was thrown out. I managed to shift my body so, instead of rolling toward the wall, I rolled parallel to it."

He nodded and patted my hand lightly. "You see how strong the instinct of self-preservation is?"

"It doesn't make sense."

"Yes, it does."

"No," I contradicted. "I really wanted to die those two years I spent in the hospital."

"You kept telling yourself that until you believed

it. You nurtured your guilt complex until it became so all consuming, you could think of nothing else. You want to live, Betty, and you're going to live. A long and happy life. And it's what your parents would have wanted for you."

"Yes," I admitted. "They were warm, generous-hearted people."

"And tell yourself this. The fault of that accident lay with whoever left the box and wire so carelessly exposed. Especially since the connections had been made."

"I know that, but if I had walked, in ladylike fashion, instead of breaking into that wild run, Mama and Papa might well be alive today."

"First of all, you must stop thinking that. Others have had the same thought and destroyed themselves with it. Unless you stop it, you'll do the same thing."

"I suppose you're right, but it isn't easy."

"Just as difficult as being confined to your wheelchair," he admitted.

"Suppose I do succeed in getting that thought out of my mind, will I ever walk?"

"We'll work on the theory that you will." He got on one knee and opened his bag. He seemed to be fumbling about for something. His hat lay on the ground near the back of the chair. He leaned forward to pick it up.

I felt a sharp twinge in my leg and cried out.

"What is it?" he asked.

"I don't know. Something—my leg seemed to hurt. At least, there was some sort of sensation in it."

"Good," he smiled.

"What's good about it?" I asked.

He took a small padding of gauze from his bag and without any apology, lifted my skirt and touched my leg with it. Then he showed me the wad of gauze. It contained a bright stain of blood. He smiled at my confusion.

"I'm sorry I caused bloodstains on your stocking too, Betty."

"What happened?"

"I jabbed your leg with a needle. You felt it."

"Strange," I said, still puzzled. "I never felt anything before."

"Didn't you refuse to let them make the necessary tests?"

"How do you know?"

"I sent a telegram to Dr. Beardsley asking for a complete history of you. He replied with a long telegram furnishing me with information. Among the things in it was the fact that you refused all tests."

"I tried to stand in the privacy of my room," I countered.

"What happened?"

"I fell and had to pull myself up and back into bed. It was horrible."

"That was unfair to you and your doctor. However, I admire your spirit, though not your false pride."

"Do you believe I'll walk again?" I asked hopefully, for suddenly, without having any particular reason, I wanted to become a whole person.

"I make no promises. The rock that crushed your legs also damaged the nerves. For some time you were paralytic. But the nerves healed."

"Then why can't I walk?"

"For one thing, the muscles have grown ineffective from disuse. If you'd allowed them to treat you, proper exercise, massage and other treatments would have helped restore them—with your will and cooperation, of course. But you refused, and the muscles went back to sleep."

"Yet you offer me hope?"

"Because you exhibited pain when I jabbed your leg. However, it may be the muscles have atophied. We're not going to think about that though. We're going to start our therapy with the idea it will be successful because you felt pain from the jab of the needle. Just don't expect success overnight."

"I'll cooperate in every way possible, Doctor," I said.

"Splendid," he replied. "I'll take you back now. I suggest we keep our plan about helping you to regain the use of your legs a secret. At least, for the time being."

At first, I was disappointed, for I wished everyone at the house to know I was going to do everything he suggested so that I'd be completely well again. But then I saw the logic of his suggestion. If his therapy failed, no one would know my disappointment or heartache.

"A splendid idea," I said brightly. "I'd just love to surprise them by standing and walking across the room."

"Concentrate on that and you'll do it. Don't let either the length of time it may take or your first faltering efforts disappoint you."

EIGHT

Supper was a pleasant affair. I'd sent word to the quarry through Lew, inviting Harley and Dudley to join us. Strange how my interest in those about me heightened after Dr. Egan's visit. I suppose strange wasn't the proper word because it seemed as if a whole new world had suddenly opened to me. I hadn't realized how much inside myself I'd lived and how selfish I'd become, thinking of no one's welfare but my own.

Afterward, we repaired to the drawing room. Both fireplaces glowed, sending a comfortable and welcome warmth through the room, dispelling the damp caused by a sudden summer rain which fell heavily. It did nothing to lower our spirits, for the conversation was cheerful, lacking only Uncle Elijah's hearty laughter. He was still confined upstairs.

I'd asked Dudley to wheel me back to the drawing room at supper's end. The others followed, grouping around the fireplace just inside the room. I told Maggie she might have the evening until I was ready to retire, to herself. She thanked me and headed for the stairs, going on, I suppose, to her room for some well-deserved rest, free for awhile of the responsibility of keeping a watchful eye on me.

I had Dudley wheel me to the far end of the room where the second fireplace was located. He sat in a chair facing me, a suitable distance from the fireplace. I recalled that he was a widower, now living with his mother who was, just as I, wheelchair confined.

"She's bright and cheerful," he said, in answer to my question as to her well-being. "However, the rheumatism has crippled her so badly, the doctor says she'll never walk again."

"Is there something I can do to make her a little more comfortable?" I asked.

His face lit up hopefully. "I believe the nicest thing you could do, Miss Betty, would be to pay her a visit. She still remembers how thoughtful you were each time you came to the village."

I prodded my memory. "I'm embarrassed, Dudley. I can't remember ever doing anything for your mother. I know Mama paid her frequent visits, but I went with her only seldom."

"True," he agreed. "But whenever you passed the house, you always waved to her and even blew her a kiss sometimes."

I was astounded that such a little thing had held such significance. "Did that mean so much to her?"

He smiled. "Indeed it did. You were such a bright, cheerful girl, with a smile for everybody. And when you're confined, as she is, the slightest thoughtfulness is a gift."

"You know," I said pensively, "until you mentioned it just now, I'd forgotten that girl. Have I changed so much, Dudley?"

"Why shouldn't you have changed?" he asked sympathetically. "No one could witness what you did without something happening to them inside."

"That's what I thought," I said. "But I realize now, I was using my condition to excuse myself for what happened."

"Nonsense, Miss Betty," he said, refuting my statement.

"Don't condone my behavior, Dudley," I said. "I know, since my return, I've been as difficult as I was in the hospital. However, Dr. Egan brought me to my senses. At least, he made a start."

"He's very dedicated. We're fortunate to have such a good doctor up here in the wilderness."

"Yes," I agreed. "He could become wealthy in a short time with a large-city practice."

"Oh, he's a doctor through choice," Dudley informed, warning to the subject. "He's independently wealthy, you know."

"I didn't know," I said, though I couldn't help but smile as I recalled the large fee he'd charged me.

"What are you smiling at?" he asked.

"I was just thinking of something he did," I said. "I will say he has a way of bringing an uncooperative patient to his senses."

"He's a kindly man without making it appear so," Dudley said. "He's going to build a small hospital in the village—or did you know that?"

"I am surprised," I said. "He didn't mention it."

"He wouldn't," Dudley said. "He's modest. I will say this, Miss Betty—and not feel I'm talking out of turn since you're taking an interest in the quarry. He did question me as to estimates on the marble. He wanted it for the facade. When I informed him of the cost, he decided it would be wiser to put the money into equipment which would be more beneficial to the patients."

I nodded understandingly. "I agree. However, what a nice gesture it would be if he'd allow us to present the marble for the facade. Certainly, the quarry would be unworkable were it not for the people who are content to live in the small village miles from anywhere."

Dudley's lean features lit up. "Miss Betty, he would appreciate it so much."

I looked doubtful. "I wonder."

"What do you mean?"

"He can be difficult."

Dudley smiled. "So can you, Miss Betty, if you'll pardon my saying so. A clash of personalities, so to speak."

I smiled in turn. "I suppose you're right. But there is a solution if you'll go along with it."

"Just name it. I'm your servant."

"No, Dudley," I contradicted. "You're my friend."

"Thank you, Miss Betty. I know your father considered me so."

"And now you know I do. Therefore, as my friend, please talk with the good Dr. Egan. Tell him we wish to contribute our share to the hospital and add that I'll be deeply hurt if he refuses."

"If he's at home when I go back tonight, I'll tell him."

"Whatever you wish," I said. "And the next time you come for dinner, I would like your mother to accompany you."

"Thank you, Miss Betty. I'm sure she would if it were possible, but her slightest movement causes pain and the jouncing she'd get in the carriage would be sheer agony for her."

"Of course," I said. "In that case, I will visit her whenever I am in town and she feels up to seeing me."

"That will be wonderful news for me to bring back to her," he said.

"Does she have someone caring for her?" I asked.

"I pay a widow woman in the village—a Mrs. Grenow—to be with her. Mrs. Grenow comes in each morning and stays until I return at night. I know she would like to make her home with us because it would be cheaper for her, but it wouldn't look right, for I'm a widower and no one will ever take the place of my beloved Erica."

"I understand," I said.

"Would you think me rude if I left now?" he asked.

"The rain is coming down hard and the roads will be deep with mud."

"Indeed not," I said. "I'm sorry to have brought you out on such a night."

"We had no warning of it," he said, dismissing the inconvenience with a barely perceptible shrug of his shoulders.

"Suppose you wheel me over to the others," I said, "so you may say your good-nights to them. Tell your mother I'll pay her a visit very soon."

"Thank you, Miss Betty. I will."

He wheeled me over to the family still grouped about the fireplace. Harley sat to one side of it, but he and Lew arose at our approach.

I said, "Dudley is leaving. I didn't realize a storm was on the way or I'd have postponed the supper for another evening."

"Until you mentioned it," Harley said gallantly, "I'd forgotten it was raining."

"Thank you," I said, smiling. I was quiet then until Dudley paid his respects and departed.

Aunt Liz said, "He's such an admirable person. So devoted to his mother."

"He should think of the future," Rena said irreverently. "His mother won't live forever."

Aunt Liz gave her a chiding look. "What a horrible thing to say."

Rena shrugged. "Perhaps it's horrible, but it's the truth."

"I don't think Dudley would allow any woman to come between him and his love for the quarry," Harley said, his smile tolerant. "Did you know he's there all night sometimes?"

Aunt Liz looked horrified. "You mean he leaves his mother alone?"

"The Widow Grenow never leaves Mrs. Seaver until Dudley comes home," Harley informed.

"Is there a romance brewing?" Lew asked quizzically.

The conversation had taken a turn I didn't like. It was as if Lew was ridiculing Dudley. I said, "He still mourns the loss of his beloved wife."

"Yes, he does," Harley agreed. "Also, he's devoted to his mother who looks old beyond her years because of her pain-wracked body."

"It's heartening to hear a man speak well of another," Rena said, her soft brown eyes openly admiring Harley.

He smiled in recognition of the compliment. I was pleased to hear her speak a few words in praise of Dudley. I only hoped Lew would take no offense at her manner which I considered rather flirtatious. But Lew's smile dispelled any uneasiness I felt. I don't mean that he condoned her misbehavior, if it could be construed as such, but apparently he was highly tolerant of it. I suppose because he knew she truly loved him, but was one of those women who had to have constant admiration from the opposite sex.

I decided to switch the conversation and said, "I hope Uncle Elijah is better this evening."

"I'm sure he is," Aunt Liz spoke affirmatively, "because he's thoroughly disgusted that the doctor won't allow him downstairs. I only wish he could see the change in you, Betty."

Lew regarded me speculatively. "I must say, Cousin, you seem to have come alive in the last twenty-four hours. Any particular reason?"

Rena gave me a knowing side glance as she said, "The reason could well be one very handsome Dr. Jeffrey Egan."

Harley regarded me with mock dismay. "You mean I have a rival?"

"You're both being foolish," I said, smiling tolerantly. "The only thing which happened today was that Dr. Egan persuaded me to stop feeling sorry for myself."

Harley sobered. "I wouldn't say you felt sorry for yourself."

"I would," I said with a smile, "because I did. I still feel I was guilty of gross carelessness, but I'm not going to shut myself up and condemn myself to a life of loneliness and self-pity. Dr. Egan convinced me of the foolishness of that."

"What else did he convince you of?" Rena asked,

eyeing me mischievously.

"That I'm a woman and should start acting like one," I said firmly.

"Well-spoken," Harley said. "I was just thinking —if you'd like to pay your respects to your uncle, I'll gladly carry you upstairs."

"Thank you, Harley, but I wouldn't let you," I said.

"Please do, dear." Aunt Liz's face had brightened at the suggestion. "Elijah would like to see you. Particularly tonight. You have such an 'alive' look."

"Very well," I said, "but on one condition. That Lew carries my chair upstairs. At the landing, I will get into it and wheel myself into Uncle Elijah's and Aunt Liz's suite."

"Fair enough," Harley said. He arose and came over to me. "You'll have to put your arms around my neck."

"That shouldn't be any hardship," Rena said, softening her words with a smile.

"I'd much rather carry my cousin than the awkward old chair," Lew grumbled.

"I don't blame you," Harley chuckled. "But I spoke first."

I laughed at their good-natured banter and slipped my arms about Harley's neck. He carried me gently and effortlessly, giving evidence of a strong, muscular body. The stairs were many and he insisted the others precede us, stating he didn't wish an audience. I was grateful, knowing he did it for fear I'd be self-conscious about being carried up. Up until today I had been, but I'd made up my mind, after Dr. Egan left, I'd accept my disability, but do all in my power to overcome it. And so I felt not the slightest discomfiture, except for a few words spoken by Harley in an undertone so the others wouldn't hear.

"You're very beautiful tonight," he said. "So beautiful I can't resist saying you hold a very special place in my heart."

"Surely you're not serious," I replied, coloring under his intent gaze.

"And why not?"

"I've known you since I was a child," I said, keeping my tone light. "Your romantic escapades were common gossip among the servants."

Far from being offended, a devilish gleam came into his eyes as he said, "How could it be? I've never been the escort of a servant."

"Indeed I know that," I replied, "but they do gossip, you know, especially in front of children they believe know no better."

"Have you such a bad opinion of me?"

I smiled up at him. "On the contrary, I have tremendous respect for you. I know, since Papa's death, you're responsible for the continued success of this quarry."

"Damn the quarry," he said. "I know what I've done there. I love you, my dear . . ."

"Please, Harley," I exclaimed, thoroughly unnerved by the turn the conversation had taken. "They'll hear you."

"What if they do?" he asked.

"It's ridiculous," I said.

"You mean," he said, sobering, "it's beneath your dignity to consider me a suitor."

I scolded him with my eyes. "I mean no such thing and you know it."

"I don't," he retorted, sullenness creeping into his eyes.

"Harley," I exclaimed, "I'm a cripple."

He paused, midway up the stairs. "What the hell does that have to do with my loving you?"

"Everything—and you know it."

"Do I?"

Before I could answer, his lips touched mine and he pressed me close, holding the embrace. I couldn't fight him, not even to take my arms from around his neck, lest I throw him off balance. So I was helpless until he broke off the embrace. I looked up to see Rena and Lew regarding us, both giving evidence of their startlement which, in no way, exceeded mine.

"Please don't be angry," he said. "But even if you are, it was worth it."

"Don't let it happen again," I replied coldly.

"Not until you give permission." His manner was teasing, but I was in no mood for it and I made no answer.

He resumed his ascent of the stairs and deposited me gently in the chair.

Lew said, "Would you like me to wheel you?"

"Yes, please," I replied, "since I don't know which suite Aunt Liz and Uncle Elijah are occupying."

"It's the one your parents used," Rena said.

"In that case, I can wheel myself," I replied.

I was startled, but managed not to show it. Also, a little annoyed that my aunt and uncle had chosen, of the several suites in the Castle, to select that one. I suppose because it was the most ornate.

Aunt Liz was awaiting me at the door. She stepped into the room, allowing me free entry. Uncle Elijah was ensconced in a large, overstuffed chair, his ailing foot heavily bandaged and resting on a large pillow. He looked quite elegant in a silk paisley dressing gown. His silver mane of hair glistened in the lamplight and his eyes sparkled at sight of me.

"Thank you, my dear, for coming up to pay me a visit," he said, his voice booming through the room. "I've been champing at the bit up here by myself, wondering what's going on."

"It's good to see you, Uncle," I said. I'd wheeled myself over to his side and I leaned forward to lightly kiss his cheek.

"That's my girl," he said, patting my hand which rested on the wheel. "Liz tells me you're not mad at Dr. Egan any more."

I smiled. "Perhaps it wasn't so bad, his making me angry. It really woke me up to what I was turning into. I'm going to change, Uncle Elijah."

He regarded me closely. "You have already. There's a warm glow in your eyes that wasn't in evidence when you returned."

Rena said, "Could it be Betty's fallen in love with the good doctor?"

"Don't be ridiculous," I scoffed. "I scarcely know him and I'm not one of those silly women who fall in love with their doctors."

"You could do worse, my dear," Aunt Liz said in that complaisant way of hers.

Lew nodded soberly and said, "Two fortunes are better than one."

"I think that's very crude," I said, making no attempt to keep the sharpness out of my voice.

"So do I," Harley said. "Dr. Egan's work with the sick is the talk of the village, particularly since no one thought Dr. Reed could be replaced."

"I understand he's interested in building a hospital," I said. "I told Dudley to inform him we'd present marble for the facade."

"That's mighty generous of you, Betty," Harley said.

"I don't think so," I said. "Particularly since he's going to use his personal fortune to build the hospital."

Lew bowed low. "Be assured, my dear cousin, if I had even a small amount of your wealth, I too would contribute generously to the erection of the edifice."

"I shall see that some of the marble is given in your name," I said.

"Please don't," he replied, in a more serious vein. "It would be a mockery."

"I don't agree," I said.

"Lew is right," Uncle Elijah spoke up. "It would be a joke among the villagers who know we live here on your largess."

"I want you here." I spoke in all seriousness.

"We know you do, my dear," Aunt Liz said. "And we're grateful."

"I don't want you to be grateful—just happy. I'll do everything to ensure your happiness."

"The best way of doing that," Uncle Elijah said, "is to continue to be as bright and cheerful as you are tonight."

"I give you my word," I said, smiling.

This time it was he who leaned forward and kissed my cheek. And so did Aunt Liz. I found their gesture most heartening. I also realized I was fatigued. It had been a good day and a full one.

"Will you please call Maggie now?" I asked Aunt Liz.

"Certainly," she said and went off to summon her.

Before I could say a word, Lew had swooped me up in his arms. "I'll do the honors this time," he said.

I was relieved because I didn't want Harley to murmur further endearments, or to attempt another kiss. I wanted no scene or any subsequent embarrassments. It had been a happy day for me and I wanted to keep it so. I still couldn't take him seriously. I felt he was flattering me, knowing his reputation for having a way with the opposite sex. Nonetheless, his gesture had annoyed me, for I'd never given him the slightest encouragement or hint I nurtured a special affection for him. I also wondered what Rena and Lew were thinking. I knew they'd witnessed the kiss, for their startlement was evident. I hoped they didn't think I'd encouraged it. I also hoped I wasn't being too critical of Harley. The gesture may have been merely to make me feel a whole woman. With that thought in mind, I dismissed the incident from my mind.

At the foot of the stairs, Maggie took over. I bade the others good night and she wheeled me to my room. I performed my ablutions and accepted her help in silence, for I was truly weary. Yet it was a wonderful feeling, for I was asleep minutes after my head settled on the pillow.

NINE

The next morning I breakfasted in my room because Aunt Liz sent word through Lorette she had a message for me from Dudley. Maggie requested permission to breakfast in the kitchen and I gladly gave it, asking that she tell Aunt Liz I'd be glad to see her. And so, though she disdained a second breakfast, she did sip a cup of coffee while I ate.

"I've always been an early riser," she said, "and I was taking my morning walk when Dudley came along."

"Wasn't it wet outside?" I asked, remembering the rainstorm.

"I wore overshoes," she said, in that crisp, nononsense manner of hers. "Rain or shine I wear them here because the dew doesn't lift until late morning."

"I know." I spread orange marmalade on my toast and took a bite, savoring its tart flavor.

Aunt Liz said, "Dear, let me have the other half of that slice of toast and spread some marmalade on it, please. Gildy does make delicious marmalade. Delicious everything, I might say, to be fair about it."

"I agree. And I'm afraid I'm going to get fat eating like this and sitting in this chair."

"Then the thing to do is convince yourself you'll get out of it at the earliest opportunity," Aunt Liz said.

I spread marmalade on the toast and handed it to her. She bit into it and very inelegantly patted her abdomen, indicating the degree to which she relished it.

"I understand you have a message from Dudley," I said.

"Yes, my dear," she replied. "I met him on the grounds. He was on his way here. He said that Dr. Egan would not be able to call until late afternoon. He was up most of the night with a little boy who had a severe case of croup."

"I'm sorry for the little boy. I had that when I was small and Mama and Papa spent many a sleepless night tending to me."

"It's hard on the child and a terrible worry to the parents," Aunt Liz said. "My dear, I have something else I wish to speak to you about. It concerns Elijah and me using your parents' suite. I imagine you were annoyed when you learned of it."

"Only slightly," I said, reassuring her with a smile. "It's difficult for me to change all at once. But I'm glad you're in it. Mama decorated it beautifully and it should be used."

"That isn't why we took it," she informed me. "Your bedroom adjoins it, as you know. We wanted to be close to you. I intended to nap on the chaise longue in the sitting room and leave your door open so I'd be available should you need me through the night."

"That's dear of you, Aunt Liz, and I appreciate it. But you can see how much better it is for me downstairs."

"Indeed yes. You can move about freely—in your wheelchair, that is. And no fear of heights or of

99

losing control of the chair in the upstairs hall and rolling downstairs."

"True," I kept my manner as placid as hers so I'd not reveal my chagrin at her matter-of-fact statement. "Though, in truth, I'd not thought of such a thing."

"I did," she said in that blunt way of hers. "That's why I felt I should be in the next room."

"Well, thanks to Maggie," I said, wishing to end the subject, "there's no need for your assuming that responsibility."

"She is competent," Aunt Liz agreed. "Though I still can't quite forgive her for panicking the day of the dynamite explosion."

"Please try, Aunt Liz," I said. "I've already forgotten it."

She nodded acquiescence. "I don't want to appear bossy, but I don't think it would be wise of you to have Maggie take you out this morning. Though the sun is threatening to come out, there are a few clouds still about and it's quite dampish."

"I was thinking of going into the village and ordering some new clothes. Would you care to accompany me?"

Her eyes sparkled. "I'd love to. I take it you think those other things you had made are a little frumpy. And you're right. They are. I told you that from the start."

I had to laugh. "I agree. I'm also going to pay a visit to Mrs. Seaver."

"I would like to meet Dudley's mother," Aunt Liz said. "In fact, I'd be the one to be honored. It's a little lonely up here after Boston and if I could find a lady to visit, I'm sure I'd enjoy it."

"I'm sure you'll enjoy Mrs. Seaver. She's such a cheerful person, despite the fact she's confined to a wheelchair, badly crippled with rheumatism and has been for years."

Aunt Liz stood up, eager for the trip. "How soon shall we leave?"

"I should be ready in a half hour. Rena's welcome to come if she wishes."

"She might come to the village, but I doubt she'll visit with Mrs. Seaver."

"It doesn't matter," I said. "Invite her anyway."

Aunt Liz looked her disapproval. "It will probably cost you another few frocks."

I wheeled my chair back from the table. "I can afford it. Please ask Maggie to come in and help me."

"Won't you let me, my dear?"

There was almost a pleading note in her voice. I reached up and caught her hand. "Thank you, Aunt Liz. Your offer means a great deal. But you'd be too kind to me and Maggie lets me do as much by myself as possible. It's the way I want it."

Aunt Liz gave a firm nod of her head. "Good. You'll be out of that chair yet."

I wondered what she'd have said if she knew such was my intent. I might not succeed, but if I failed to walk again, it wouldn't be because I hadn't tried with all the will I possessed. I intended to abide by Dr. Egan's suggestion, however, that I take no one into my confidence. It was wise, for the surprise when I arose from my chair and took a few steps would be monumental.

"How is Uncle Elijah this morning?"

"Much better, I'd say. Though he's not to come

downstairs or even walk on that foot until the doctor gives the word."

"I hope he'll obey."

"So do I. But he's growling like a grizzly. Not only because of his confinement, but his diet. However, I just listen, agree with everything he says, then tell him to behave himself and not stir from the chair without the doctor's say-so."

I smiled. "I guess he needs a stern hand at the helm."

"Of course he takes it out on Lew, telling him he isn't looking after the horses or the stable as he should. And he isn't," she added, with a knowing nod of her head.

"I'm going to hire a stableman when we get in the village," I said. "It's important for the horses to receive proper care."

"Your uncle will feel hurt," Aunt Liz said.

I hit upon an idea to pacify him. "I'll tell the stableman he's to take orders from Uncle Elijah. You know, Auntie, that work is too hard for him. It may even have brought on the attack of gout."

"I agree the work is a lot, but Elijah felt it was one way we could show our appreciation for our being here."

"I need you," I said simply. "What more can I say?"

Aunt Liz cupped my face between her hands. "My dear, you are a true daughter to your parents." She bent and kissed my cheek. "I'll tell Rena she may come with us if she wishes."

"And send Maggie in," I called to her.

And Rena did come, though she asked to be taken directly to the milliner's, stating she would meet us at Mrs. Adams. I fancied quite a millinery bill, but I was in an expansive mood and I didn't mind, wanting only contentment for everyone.

Mrs. Seaver was overjoyed at seeing us. She was painfully thin, with hollow cheeks and sunken eyes, but there was a merry glint in them and her smile was animated. I brought her a soft cashmere shawl of a blue that matched her eyes. I'd purchased it for Mama and had intended to present it to her on her anniversary. Needless to say, it still lay in its beribboned box. Mrs. Seaver was overjoyed at sight of the pretty wrappings and asked if she might refrain from opening it until Dudley could see it. I consented, for I also had a gift-wrapped package for him—a pipe I'd purchased for Papa. I handed over both gifts to Mrs. Grenow, a competent, pleasant-faced woman, who placed them in a prominent spot on the parlor table.

We reminisced for awhile and I was amazed at how much Mrs. Seaver knew about me. Apparently, Mama had told her, in great detail, about my schooling and my hobbies. She brought Mama into the conversation frequently and was especially pleased to learn Aunt Liz was her sister. They carried on a lively conversation and when I stated I must leave, they both seemed reluctant to have the visit end. I suggested to Aunt Liz that she remain there until I conducted my business with the dressmaker. She was overjoyed once she was reassured Mrs. Seaver wouldn't be too tired.

Lew had remained in the carriage, but Aunt Liz called him in and he carried me out. I must say that, though indolent, he exercised great care in handling me and I expressed my gratitude to him. He smiled that lazy smile of his, took my hand and pressed it gently to his lips. It was his way of thanking me and I was warmed by the gesture.

Rena was already at Mrs. Adams who was delighted at seeing me and more than pleased that I'd decided on a change of fashion, telling me I was too young for the frills and furbelows and, with my figure, I should wear clothes that showed it to advantage. I assured her I would carry out her suggestion and I did, surprising her pleasantly with my selections and causing Rena's eyebrows to raise, for the decolletage of one gown was quite daring. I thought I might never wear it, nevertheless I enjoyed making the choice if for no other reason than to view Rena's shocked amazement.

Once again, Lew carried me back to the carriage. We stopped by Mrs. Seaver's for Aunt Liz. Mrs. Seaver nodded to me from the window. I knew that the act of even raising her hand was painful. I waved to her, but had to prompt Rena to do so and was annoyed at the lackadaisical manner in which she responded. But Aunt Liz more than made up for it and was quite animated from her visit, talking all the way home, informing us she intended to visit Mrs. Seaver every day, weather permitting. Lew stated he had no intention of driving her back and forth, which statement reminded me I'd forgotten to hire a stableman.

"I knew you would," Aunt Liz said. "Who could think of such a mundane thing when selecting a new wardrobe, so I asked Mrs. Seaver to have Dudley do it. I knew I couldn't depend on Lew to take me back and forth and goodness knows when Elijah will be able to."

"Soon, I hope," I said. "But I'm grateful for your thoughtfulness."

"It was partially selfish," she stated in that blunt way of hers. "But I told Elijah you were hiring a stableman provided he would assume responsibility. It made him feel important, so the stableman will have to take orders from Elijah."

"That was tactful of you, Auntie," I complimented her.

"With a man, my dear, one has to be," she said matter-of-factly.

"Guess who I met in the village," Rena said.

"Tell us and save us the trouble," Aunt Liz said tartly.

"Harley Denison," Rena said, turning in the front seat to regard me.

"Why wasn't he at the quarry attending to matters there?" Aunt Liz asked.

"He had business at the bank," Rena replied. "Also, he had to send some telegrams. But he took the time to bring me into Gafferty's ice cream parlor for a soda."

"I don't approve of that," Aunt Liz said. "You're a married woman."

"Lew doesn't mind, do you, darling?" Rena asked.

"Not with Harley," Lew replied. "But just as a matter of curiosity, what did you talk about?"

"Romance," she said, giggling.

"Whose" he asked.

She smiled mischievously. "I think he is enamored of one Betty Bowen. He could talk of no one else. Betty's lovely, silken blond hair and how silvery it looks when the sun touches it. Betty's pale skin as smooth as a rose petal. Betty's soft, cultured voice which . . .?"

"Stop it, Rena," I said sternly. "I don't like being made a fool of."

"Maybe I'm jealous," she said, eyeing me appraisingly.

"I think you're disgusting," I said. "Even if Harley did make any comments about me, I'm sure he didn't expect you'd turn them into ridicule."

She was piqued at my rebuff. "He meant them as compliments. And so do I. You're as touchy now as you were the day you came home."

"She has reason to be," Aunt Liz scolded. "You're being rude."

Rena gave a defiant toss of her head. "Fiddle-faddle."

"Shut up, Rena," Lew said. "We both know in what high regard Harley holds Betty. If we didn't before, after last night we do."

"What does last night have to do with it?" Aunt Liz asked.

Rena's smile was vindictive. "Lew and I saw Harley kiss Betty most fervently while carrying her upstairs. Betty made no protest."

"I wasn't in a very good position to," I said, thoroughly uncomfortable under Aunt Liz's scrutinizing gaze.

She said, "I hope you won't be offended, my dear, if I ask if there is something serious between you and Harley."

"You may ask me anything you wish regarding Harley or anyone else," I said quietly. "As to Harley—or anyone else—I have no romantic entanglements, nor do I intend to have any, crippled as I am."

"Just because your legs can no longer serve you," Aunt Liz said, "is no reason why you shouldn't fall in love."

"You may be right, Auntie. But I'm not in love with Harley Denison. I'm sure you know what a flirt he is."

"I do. That's way I was a little taken aback by such news."

"It's not news. It's not even true. Now suppose we drop the subject."

"A worthy idea." Aunt Liz settled back on the seat alongside me, seemingly relieved. However, I noticed her give me a few cautious glances from time to time and I thought I detected doubt in her eyes.

Maggie, wheeling my chair out onto the porch, was a welcome sight as we drew up to the door. The expedition, which had started out on a light note, left me a little distraught. I was glad there'd be time for a nap before Dr. Egan arrived, for I felt great need of it. I wished to be refreshed when he came because I sensed he would begin the therapy of getting me on my feet today. I only hoped neither Rena nor Lew would mention the incident of Harley kissing me. I didn't want the good doctor to think me a fickle character. I was certain he was as aware of Harley's reputation with the ladies as I. I didn't flatter myself his feelings toward me were different. I still believed he'd kissed me to make me think I was equally as desirable as a woman who had the use of her legs. But I didn't need to be convinced in such fashion and if he attempted to do so a second time, I would tell him.

TEN

It was almost three o'clock when Dr. Egan arrived. He went upstairs to see Uncle Elijah, but was there only briefly. Again, I excused Maggie and awaited him in the den. He entered, a grin widening his face and came directly over to my chair.

"You look well today," he said.

"I'm refreshed after a nap," I said. "And most eager to begin the therapy."

"Splendid. We'll start at once. You need a wrap though. There's a little chill in the air after the storm."

I reached over and picked a paisley shawl from a chair. "I expected you'd say that and having been out already today, I know it's the truth."

He took the shawl from me, draped it across my shoulders and started wheeling me toward the hall. "I know you've been to the village. I stopped in to see how Mrs. Seaver was doing. Your visit made her day one to remember."

"She'll have others. Aunt Liz thoroughly enjoyed visiting with her and intends to return each day, weather permitting."

"That's good of her," Dr. Egan said. He wheeled me through the door which Lorette held open for him. He maneuvered the wheel chair carefully down the stairs and pushed it toward the path flanked by the marble columns. "Any particular place you'd like me to wheel you to?"

I remembered the tomb and the marble angel. "Yes. Follow the path, please, until I show you where to veer off."

He did so, heeding my directions until we were headed directly for the tomb. "Stop a short distance from it, will you, please?"

He did and we observed the structure in silence.

Dr. Egan broke it, saying, "That's quite a mausoleum."

"Do you like it?"

"The marble in it is exquisite, as you know. I think I'd have preferred the angel on the ground rather than perched on the top. It spoils the lines."

"It does indeed. But Papa planned it that way and I'm reluctant to have the angel taken down and placed in front."

"The open top is unusual too."

"And not particularly appealing. Besides which it will catch fallen leaves and dead branches of the overhanging trees."

"Does anything about it look familiar?" I asked.

Dr. Egan studied it a moment, then exclaimed, "The angel! It has your face. Whose idea was that?"

"Aunt Liz's, I think."

"Why?" His voice evidenced his disapproval.

"She thought it would be a nice touch. I wasn't expected to get well. Reports from the hospital were discouraging and so they prepared for what they believed to be the inevitable."

"I wouldn't blame you if you had the thing torn down."

"I couldn't. My grandparents' remains were disinterred from the family grave and placed there. My parents' are there also. There is even a niche for me, with my name and date of birth already on the marble plaque."

Dr. Egan said ruminatively, "They were leaving nothing to chance, were they?"

"I was angry at first, but I'm not now. Aunt Liz is a forceful person, but also a kindly one. I'm sure Mrs. Seaver convinced you of that."

He was standing alongside my chair, his attention now directed to me. "I'm sure your aunt meant no harm."

"How is my uncle?"

"Coming along nicely. It was a mild attack. I'm scaring him more than anything. He does have to take it easy from now on though. More for his heart than the gout. He can no longer attend the horses or the stable."

"I don't want him to," I said. "Dudley will get me a stableman and I'll let Uncle Elijah supervise him."

Dr. Egan nodded approval. "That will satisfy him."

"Doctor, I understand you have plans for building a hospital in the village."

He smiled. "Dudley stopped by last night and told me of your offer. It's most generous."

"Will you honor me by accepting marble for the facade?"

"I'll be the grateful one and I do accept. Now I suggest I wheel you just beyond the tomb. I see an old apple tree there, with gnarled branches that are low and would be a good support for you."

He wheeled me directly to the spot. Fortunately, the ground was level and one branch only waist high.

"We're completely concealed here and it's a perfect place to begin unobserved."

His hands enclosed my waist, but I gripped the chair arms tightly. "I can't. I know I can't. Let's forget it, Doctor."

"We'll not forget it." As he spoke, he was raising me and I had to release my hold of the chair. "Put your hands on that branch. Rest your arms on it. You don't have to move."

"I couldn't if I wanted to," I exclaimed breathlessly. Whether from my exertions or fear, I didn't know, but my body was suddenly soaked with perspiration. Then he released his hold and I was hanging on to the branch for dear life. My body felt many times heavier than it was.

"Raise your arms and just hold on with your hands." His voice, though quiet, held a commanding tone.

I did so, though I was now trembling from head to foot.

"Now lift your hands."

"I can't."

"You can. Lift them."

I obeyed, but my legs were wobbling and everything started to spin. I was about to collapse. He was at my side and he caught hold of me. I rested my head against his shoulder, for my breath was rapid and I felt quite weak and helpless, but he continued to hold my dead weight for at least another minute. Then, still supporting me, he shifted his position slightly, so that he could lift me and place me gently in the chair. I leaned my head against its cushioned back. I was thoroughly spent.

"You did well," he said.

"I didn't prove I could walk or that my legs would support me."

"You stood unaided, even though only for a moment," he said. "Beginning today, I want you to start massaging your legs gently. From the thighs to the knees, from the knees to the ankles whenever you have the time. Preferably when you're alone. I still want to keep this therapy secret. Watch what I do so you'll know the proper procedure."

He demonstrated the precise method of massage, first on his left leg, then on his right. After that, he extracted a promise I would never let a day go by without exercising the muscles through massage. That, along with practice out here, and he felt I had an excellent change of walking again.

When he finished the demonstration, he eased himself to the ground and sat at my feet, using the tree trunk as a support. I closed my eyes and over a half hour passed before I opened them. When I looked down at him, he smiled and nodded reassuringly.

I said, "I'm going to dread this each day."

"It's rough," he admitted. "But you can do it. The muscle massage is most important. Don't neglect it."

"I promise."

"Would you like to go back to the house or shall we continue our tour?"

"Would you care to visit the quarry?"

"Indeed, yes. The place fascinates me. And with you, I'll have an excuse for being there."

"Then let that be our next stop. I'll take you on a guided tour."

I directed Dr. Egan back to the path, partially concealed by shrubbery. This time I remembered exactly where it was. I heard him give a muffled exclamation as he pushed the shrubbery aside and saw the steepness of it.

"Sure you can hang on?" he asked. "You're tired, you know."

"Not that tired," I said. Nor was I. At least, that's what I told myself. Later, I knew I'd not allowed myself to reveal fatigue. I wished to remain in his company as long as possible. It was selfish, I knew, for he was a busy man. But his presence cheered me and I was pleased to have the excuse of showing him the quarry.

Dudley came out to greet us as Dr. Egan rolled my chair in the direction of the old shed at the base of the quarry. As always, he wore his green eyeshade, paper wrapped around his cuffed sleeves to prevent soil, and a pencil tucked over one ear. His features broke into a smile at sight of us.

"Nice to see you, Miss Betty," he said. "You too, Doctor."

"Thank you," Dr. Egan said. "Miss Betty offered to take me here and I jumped at the opportunity."

"Nice to have you," Dudley said. "As you know, I'm the bookkeeper so I'm not so good at explaining things. Reggie takes care of getting the marble out of the ground and Harley makes sure it goes to the place where we get the most money for it."

"Are Harley or Reggie about?" I asked. The quarry was, as always, a scene of much activity. The many men swarming over one area where the blasting had sent down an avalanche of dirt and rock seemed dwarfed against the high wall of the quarry. Just now they were engaged in clearing the dirt and rock loosened by the explosion. Once that was disposed of, they'd be close to the surface of the blue marble. I felt fortunate I wasn't part of the avalanche because the blast which had sent it cascading down the side of the quarry had been the one set off on the day Maggie and I had chosen to go there.

Dudley gave orders to a man nearby to summon both Reggie and Harley.

Harley arrived first, greeted me and shook hands with Dr. Egan. His manner with both of us was friendly, but businesslike, and I felt relieved. I wanted no further display of warmth or affection on his part.

"We've made a find," Harley went on, for Dr. Egan's benefit. "A rare marble of dark blue streaked with crimson. It makes beautiful archway entrances for important buildings, it has a striking effect when a large room, like that of a museum, or palace, is lined with it. We'll have no trouble selling it, only in getting it out of the ground fast enough to meet our orders."

Reggie, puffing from his brisk run from the far end of the quarry, hurried up to us. After greeting us, Dr. Egan asked about the procedure for getting marble out of the quarry. Harley motioned for Reggie to explain.

"It's simple, Doctor," he said. "First, we blast the surface dirt and rock clear. Then we level off the top layer of marble. That done, we put the machines to work."

"No more blasting?" Dr. Egan asked. He was plainly interested.

"Never! Any further explosions would crack the marble, ruin big pieces of it. We create a floor, as I said. Then the channeling machines—that's one over there... Come, I'll show you."

It was Harley who wheeled my chair now. We came to a halt beside the idle machine, a huge contrivance operated by steam manufactured in a large upright boiler. I remembered when I was small, how mortally afraid I was of these hissing, pounding monsters.

Reggie pointed out the cutters, arranged in gangs. "By steam pressure," he explained, "the cutters are driven into the surface of the marble to a depth of four or five inches. The machine moves in a straight line until we have rows of cuttings. Then the machine crisscrosses these cuts with more, all spaced to the size of the block we wish to extract."

"But five or six inches deep to get a chunk of marble, three or four feet thick," Dr. Egan marveled.

"It's enough. Once that work is done, we turn to the undercutting machine. That is also steam driven and it cuts through the wall of marble this time, not the floor as the channeling machine did. Now we have the blocks outlined and the cuttings begun. The next operation uses a gadder machine. This has an upright column. There's none in this part of the quarry right now, but I will be glad to show you one of them later."

"That's not necessary," Dr. Egan said. "Just tell me what a gadder does."

"The gadder uses a drill that finishes the cutting and frees the block which is then removed. Gradually, we create a new floor and the quarry is that much deeper."

Dr. Egan looked up at the perpendicular walls of marble. It was like standing at the bottom of a huge mountain with one side sheared off. "I can't imagine how much marble you took out of this one quarry," he said. "I've never seen anything like this before. It's a marvel to me, speaking as a medical man, that there aren't all kinds of severe accidents among your workmen."

"Because we insist on their being careful rather than fast," Harley explained, "we have few accidents."

"The last one was almost three years ago," Reggie said. "Maggie Morfit's husband was killed when he fired up one of the boilers too much and it blew up. It was his fault. The quarry was not held to blame."

"Even so, Betty's father took good care of Maggie," Harley said.

"Thanks very much," Dr. Egan said. "I'd best get Miss Betty back now before she becomes too tired."

"Come by any time." Harley shook hands with him again. "Next time perhaps all the machines will be in use and you can see for yourself the kind of work they do."

"If you can bear the noise," I said with a smile. "It's quite bad."

"I think it's exciting," Dr. Egan said.

"And thrilling when you find a vein of alomite," Harley said.

Dr. Egan gave a final look around, seemingly fascinated by it, then wheeled me off the floor of the quarry toward the path. He made the trip back effortlessly.

After he'd pushed aside the branches and wheeled

me onto the estate proper, he said, "I don't think you should allow Maggie to wheel you down there again. It's very treacherous."

"I shan't," I promised. He was right. If she should lose her footing and release her grip on the wheelchair, she could, in no way, be held guilty of negligence.

ELEVEN

A week passed and each day Dr. Egan came, first visiting Uncle Elijah because he'd had a slight setback. Dr. Egan confided he felt that somehow Uncle Elijah obtained some food that he was not supposed to eat. However, Uncle Elijah exclaimed indignantly he'd done no such thing since he was not allowed downstairs and Lorette was a tyrant regarding what she brought up on his tray. Not even enough to feed a sparrow.

However, his annoyance at being confined was tempered with the hiring of Chuck White as stableman. He was quiet, competent and amenable to Uncle Elijah's dictatorial manner. Aunt Liz took to Chuck immediately and, true to her word, visited Mrs. Seaver every day. Each time she returned, I could see from her conversation, the friendship deepened.

I gave Maggie more and more time to herself, for I needed time alone to carry out Dr. Egan's instructions about massaging my leg muscles. He wheeled me about the grounds each day, always heading in a different direction in case anyone might be watching from the house. However, our tour always terminated behind the mausoleum. There, he would lift me from the chair, supporting me with his hands until my arms rested on the tree branch. I had progressed to the point where I managed to take two side steps, though not lifting my feet from the ground and still maintaining a firm grip on the tree.

Each time though, I'd become perspiration-soaked and my legs would start shaking. I know I'd have collapsed except for Dr. Egan's alertness.

This day, however, the procedure differed. He faced me when he lifted me from the chair.

"Put your hands on my arms, right above the elbows. I'll keep my hands on your waist, but lightly. As I take a step backward, I want you to take one forward. When I take a second step backward, you take a second one forward. Ready?"

I nodded, frightened but determined. I took the step, but let my foot drag on the ground.

"You can do better than that," he said. "With the next step, lift your foot off the ground."

I managed, but it dropped to the ground in the same spot.

"Once again, Betty. You can do it."

And I did, though my knee buckled under me. However, he caught me and raised me gently. "Put your head on my shoulder and rest," he said. "I'll support you. I don't want you to sit down quite yet. I'm pleased with your progress and I have a feeling of certainty you're going to make it."

"I . . . hope . . . so," I said breathlessly. These sessions always left me spent, but I looked forward to them more and more, and not just because I wanted to walk. It was because of Dr. Egan. I knew I was falling in love with him. His very presence was unnerving and when he held me like this, my heart pounded madly and not just from my exertions.

"Do you feel any difference in your legs," he asked.

"I couldn't give an affirmative answer on that, Doctor, because if there is a difference, it's so faint, it's not discernible."

"Don't be discouraged," he said. "Are you faithful with the massage therapy?"

"Very," I said. "In fact, Maggie is grumbling because I give her so much free time. She feels she's not earning her wages."

"Let her grumble," he chuckled. "One of these days you'll be dismissing her."

"Suppose that day never comes," I ventured.

"Don't have such a thought," he replied.

"I can't help but think about it," I said.

Before answering, he eased me down into the chair. "Suppose you don't walk. You can still live a full life."

"In a wheelchair?" I kept my eyes lowered lest he see my discouragement revealed in them.

"Why not?" he prompted. "I know what you're thinking—of what every woman thinks. The love of a man, marriage, a family. No need to blush. It's a perfectly normal thought. And you can have all of that, even without walking. The rest of your body functions normally."

"You're talking nonsense, Doctor," I said. "I wouldn't be so presumptuous as to think a man could love me as I am. I'd be a burden and a bore."

He dropped to the ground propping himself against the tree trunk. "You sound like the young woman I talked with the first day I came here. Egocentric and filled with self-pity."

I gave an impatient toss of my head. "I don't

mean it that way. Anyway, how can you understand? You've never been confined to a wheelchair."

"No, and I pray God I never will be. But if I were, I'd like to think there was a woman in this world who could love me despite my disability."

I regarded him with surprise. "You really mean that, don't you?"

He nodded. "I love you, Betty. I hadn't meant to tell you yet because I know the anguish you're going through. I also know you're really working at trying to overcome your handicap. I respect you."

"Thank you, Doctor. You're very kind."

"I wasn't trying to be kind. Merely honest. When I say I love you, I mean it. I have no idea how you regard me."

"I have a tremendous respect for you, Doctor, both as a physician and as a man."

He was plainly rebuffed. "Thank you. I guess that puts me in my place. Forgive me for speaking out of turn."

"I didn't mean it that way," I exclaimed. "I have a deep affection for you. But I'll not let my emotion overtake my reason. I'd be a fool."

"Why not try being a woman?" he asked.

"Not a foolish one," I said, avoiding his gaze, for there was a softness in it I'd not seen before.

He shifted his position, propping himself up on one knee. "Look at me," he commanded.

I turned my head. "No. Please."

The palm of his hand touched the far side of my face and gently turned my head so as to face him. "Look at me," he repeated. "I love you, Betty. If you have any fondness for me, tell me, please. If not, I'll still come here each day to help you walk, but my manner will be that of a physician to his patient. However, if you will give me just a slight encouragement, my task will be one nurtured by love. Do I have a chance? I love you. I want you for my wife. I want you to be my companion for the rest of my days. Even if you never walk, I want that."

Though his voice was low, it was warm with love. I had to raise my eyes. They were tear-filled, but I felt no embarrassment.

"Say it, Betty. Say what is in your mind. Even if it's no, tell me."

"As I said, I have already formed a deep affection for you, Doctor, but . . ."

I never finished the sentence. He kissed away the tears that ran down my cheeks, then his lips covered mine and I tasted the salt of my own tears. The kiss was gentle and brief, but his arms enclosed me and his cheek touched mine. My hands rested in my lap. I wanted mightily to put my arms around his neck, but I dared not. I could not encourage him. Despite his declaration of love, I would not take advantage of him. As a doctor, he needed a wife who was filled with vitality and though I'd known little illness, I was helpless without my legs.

"Don't utter another word, my darling," he whispered. "I know exactly what you'll say and I don't want to hear it. I'll wear down your resistance."

He talked then of the love he bore me, of his work and how I could help him. Of other patients he'd known and treated with my handicap and how they were living a full life. And he ended on a light note, telling me I would have to forget myself and think only of his happiness. *That*, he added with mock firmness, would keep me very, very busy.

I lay awake a long time that night, trying to convince myself he was right. I felt warmed by his love and it also gave me a greater determination to make every effort to walk again. Only then would I feel justified in consenting to share his life with him. I wished mightily I could overcome that feeling of inadequacy, but I couldn't.

A drizzly rain kept me indoors the next day, but Dr. Egan came. When I addressed him formally, he insisted I use his given name. And I acquiesced. I noticed both Rena and Lew already did so and he replied, using their surnames.

That evening Reggie and his wife Teresa were dining with us. Since Jeffrey had no calls to make, I invited him to stay. However, once we were seated around the table, I sensed he'd have been much happier in his office at the village, for Teresa, a buxom woman, glowing with good health, started listing her aches and pains, plying him with questions as to their cause and what to do about them. He answered graciously and, more than once when our eyes met, he had all he could do to repress a smile. I finally succeeded in switching the conversation away from her imaginary ailments by inquiring about their son who was employed as a floorwalker in a New York department store. She launched into his career as glowingly and in as much detail as she'd done with her aches and pains.

I knew Reggie was embarrassed and I wasn't surprised when, after a decent interval following supper, he asked that they be excused. I sent Jeffrey home at the same time, well aware of the long hours he worked and that included among them was the vast amount of time he gave to helping me. I insisted he charge a fee for his services, stating he could use it for the care of indigent patients.

I asked the others to excuse me and had Maggie take me to my room. For some reason, I felt greatly fatigued. Maggie urged me to have a glass of warm milk to relax me. I consented, adding that she should have some herself. She agreed readily and after she had attended to my needs and helped me into bed, she went to the kitchen for the milk.

I lay quietly, propped on my pillows, listening to the gentle patter of rain against the quarrels. It had a soothing sound, yet I felt a sense of uneasiness. I could give no reason for it other than the fact that I was still trying to shut out Jeffrey's declaration of love. Yet my mind kept slipping back to the previous afternoon and I heard once again, Jeffrey's endearments whispered into my ear. Even thinking about it made my heart pound so I thought it would burst. I wondered how I could be so lucky. At least, I would be were I to accept his love. Yet I still held back. I wondered if it was my cowardice which sent a feeling of disquietude through me.

Maggie returned then and put an end to my musings. Just as well, I thought, for to dwell on it too much might make me weaken in my resolve to reject Jeffrey's love unless I was certain I would one day walk.

I sipped the milk slowly, but Maggie, apparently savoring it, gulped hers down.

"May I ask a question, Miss?"

"Of course, Maggie," I replied, surprised by her reticence. She, like Aunt Liz, usually spoke her mind.

"Is it serious between you and the doctor?"

"Whatever gave you such an idea?"

"The way he looks at you. And the way you don't look at him."

My smile was amused. "That doesn't make much sense," I said, though knowing it did.

She was studying me carefully. "I think he has serious intentions. And I think you more than like him."

I shrugged off the idea. "I have no patience with women who fall in love with their doctors."

She pondered that a moment. "You've scarcely reached womanhood. Just because you'll never walk doesn't mean you can't fall in love."

"Who says I'll never walk?"

"You said it, Miss Betty. More than once, I've heard you."

"I suppose I have," I admitted.

"You know you have."

I nodded. "Then all I'll say is that since I am confined to a wheelchair, I feel I'd be a burden as a wife."

"I don't believe Harley would think so," she said, a half smile on her face.

I was irritated at her boldness, but took pains to hide it. "Why do you make such a statement?"

"Gossip in the village has it that you and Harley are—well, you know, Miss."

"I don't know, Maggie. Suppose you tell me."

"Well, it's rumored your papa and mama had hoped you and Harley would one day marry. He runs the quarry so well and all that."

"I can't believe Papa and Mama had any such thought. They wouldn't expect me to marry a man just because he has an exceptional talent for management. In this case, the quarry."

"I suppose not, Miss Betty. Of course, there're other reasons for marriage."

"For me," I spoke with a quiet firmness, "there would be just one reason."

"And that, Miss Betty?"

"Mutual respect and deep love."

"Don't you respect Harley?"

"Of course I do. And I'll be eternally grateful for the way he managed the quarry during my two years in the hospital. But I don't love him."

"No, Miss Betty."

"What do you mean by that?"

"Nothing. It's just that gossip has it that he loves you."

"Harley is not the type of man who could love one woman. He's quite handsome and well aware of his attraction for the opposite sex. He'd be bored with marriage and any woman who was foolish enough to marry him would have my sympathy."

"I didn't mean to make you angry, Miss."

"Forgive me, Maggie," I said, managing a smile. "I know I'm overly sensitive about my condition. But I don't want to hear any more about village gossip concerning Harley and me."

"I placed no stock in it myself, Miss, and I told them so. Of course, I've gone in the village with your aunt these last few days because the good doctor takes up most of your time. I'd rather stay here and take care of you, but there ain't a thing for me to do."

"I don't mind your going to the village," I said. "Just don't bring me back any idle chitchat. Because that's all it is—idle gossip."

"I promise, Miss Betty. Just don't be mad at me."
"I'm not, Maggie."

And so the evening ended on a friendly note. She bade me a good night, extinguished my lamp and left the room. I heard her moving about quietly as she prepared for bed and shortly the beam of lamplight which slipped through the door faded. I closed my eyes and thought of Jeffrey and of the noble gesture he'd made in proposing to me. I still couldn't convince myself he truly loved me. Even if he did, he deserved far better than I. I had to put him out of my mind and I would. Unless, I told myself, I regained the use of my legs.

TWELVE

I awakened to a cool breeze blowing against my cheek. Though my eyes were still closed—for they were heavy with sleep—it seemed as if there was light in the room. I stirred lazily, still reluctant to raise my lids. But when I did, I blinked, protesting the light from my bedside lamp. The chair alongside the bed which Maggie used when she was in the room was empty. Puzzled, I looked about vainly for a sign of her. I noticed the door leading into the den where she slept was closed. She always left it open. Gradually, I felt faint stirrings of misgivings. I called Maggie's name, but there was no answer. I called a second time, then listened for the slightest sound of her moving about.

Only then did I realize that the light rain of early evening was now a downpour. No wonder she couldn't hear me. I noted then the casement window was open wide, yet there seemed to be something obstructing it. Something that moved with the slight breeze which came through the window. The breeze that had touched my face and awakened me. But I couldn't make out what it was. I thought, for a moment, it was a human form, except there seemed to be no depth to it. Then it moved, ever so gently. It was in the far end of the room and in a shadow.

"Who is it?" I called out. "What are you doing in here?"

There was no answer and the silence seemed to mock me. I looked at my bedside clock. It was three in the morning. I couldn't lie there in terror until daylight to see who or what was obstructing the open window which Maggie had closed because of the rain.

I knew what I must do, so I urged my torso over to the side of the bed and forced myself up to a sitting position. I slipped into my negligee which lay across the bed within easy reach. I bent forward then and slipped my right arm beneath my knees. I raised them slightly and pulled my legs off the bed. They dropped to the floor like dead weights, but I felt no pain. I felt no sensation at all. Nor did I feel discouragement. I had one aim at the moment —to get into the wheelchair. It was within arm's reach, for Maggie lifted me from it each night after bringing it as close to the side of the bed as possible.

I got a grip on it and pulled it close, though I did cast a glance over my shoulder at the form which still stood before the window. Try as I might, my eyes couldn't pierce the darkness. The only thing I knew was that the outline of the figure seemed silhouetted in the blackness surrounding it. It almost seemed to be a woman. But who? And why didn't she answer?

I turned my attention back to the chair. I didn't know how to get into it. I'd never attempted such a thing before. Fortunately my bed was high so that the part of the chair on which my feet rested could slip beneath the bed, enabling the arms to touch the bed. I fastened the brake on the chair, gripped one arm and placed my other hand on the seat. It was my intention to boost myself onto it, but when I made the effort, the chair tilted sideways and I almost fell out of bed.

I was now trembling from my efforts and, despite the damp of the night, my body was beaded with perspiration. I made a second effort and, once again, the chair started to tilt, but this time I was prepared for it and I settled back on the bed. I then hit upon the idea—one born of desperation—of placing my hand near the back of the seat and on the opposite side from the arm I gripped. That held the chair firmly and I tried once again. For one horrible moment I thought I was going overside with the chair, but I got on the edge of the chair and shifted my weight to the opposite side. But my efforts had weakened me and I had to sit there awhile. Then, resolutely, I pushed the chair back from the bed, bent forward and raised my legs with my hands, setting them on the footrests.

If it hadn't been for that form still moving listlessly before the window, I might have summoned enough energy to give a shout of glee that I'd managed to get into the chair without aid. As it was, I knew my next step was to wheel my chair over to the darkened area of the room. I began my journey, leaving the comforting lamplight and moving into what seemed to me stygian blackness. I couldn't carry a lamp, for I needed both hands to maneuver the chair. Therefore, I had to call upon what courage I possessed to advance across the room.

It took no more than a minute, yet it seemed forever. I suppose because, with each turn of the wheel, I felt as if I were advancing to my doom. I reminded myself it was a foolish thought. Nothing untoward had happened to me since the day I'd had Maggie wheel me close to the quarry and the dynamite blast had gone off, terrifying both of us.

I had now progressed to the darkened area and was but a few feet from the window and I could see what looked like a woman's dress and, in the dampness, I detected the faint odor of lavender. I was more puzzled than ever.

"Who are you?" I asked.

There was no answer. Prickles of apprehension started to rise along my arms, but I stiffened in my chair, more angry now than fearful and advanced the wheels so that my legs touched the garment. Not that they felt it, but the foot of the chair had struck the wall and the garment, pulled from its mooring, feel into my lap. It wasn't a human. It was a lady's dress—a gown, and it was a crisp fabric. With it across my lap, I wheeled my chair back to the light, thoroughly bewildered.

Not until I reached my bedside and paused, did I study the garment. But then I picked it up and held it from me. I couldn't believe my eyes. A low moan of anguish escaped me. It was the dress I was wearing the day I'd tripped over the wire and caused the dynamite explosion which had killed my parents. It was soiled and torn and copiously bloodstained. I threw it from me, for it brought back all the terrifying memories of that tragic day. I turned my chair, heading for the door. I had to learn what Maggie knew about this.

I managed to open the door silently and without any trouble, but paused when a shaft of light was revealed. I had a good view into the room and I saw a shadow on the floor of someone moving about.

Slowly and as if with an effort, the person came into view. It was Uncle Elijah. He was using a cane and his walk was halting. His free hand carried a candelabrum and he moved over to the wall of books. Holding the slim light high, he scanned a shelf of them. Apparently seeing one to his liking, he took it down and set the candle on the table. However, thrust between that book and another was a long envelope which became dislodged and fell to the long table below the shelf. He picked it up, studied it, turned it over and was about to take a piece of paper out when I made my presence known.

"I'll take that, Uncle Elijah." I spoke as I wheeled my chair into the room. "And please light the lamp on the table."

He turned so abruptly he placed the weight of his body on his sore foot, causing him to cry out in pain. In doing so, he awakened Maggie who sat up abruptly and let out a screech at the sight of him. Obviously, she was so startled she didn't realize who he was.

"It's all right, Maggie," I said. My hand was outstretched for the envelope he held.

He handed it to me, voicing neither an apology nor displaying the slightest trace of embarrassment. Then he applied a match flame to a lampwick.

I slipped the envelope into the pocket of my negligee. "What are you doing downstairs, Uncle?"

"I came down for a book," he replied as placidly as if he were discussing the weather.

"There's a bookcase filled with them in your suite," I told him.

"Is there now?" he asked, looking as innocent as a babe.

"You know there is," I said sternly. "Did you

come into my room?"

"Indeed, I did not," he said firmly, his expression now one of righteous indignation.

"He came into mine," Maggie said belligerently. She was holding the covers up tightly against her chin. "And got no business doin' so when it's my sleepin' room. Just because I work here don't mean I ain't entitled to privacy."

"Stop your bellowing," Uncle Elijah roared.

"Both of you stop shouting," I commanded. "Maggie, please get up and summon the others. I want everyone, with the exception of Lorette, down here."

"I ain't settin' foot off this couch until Mr. Pauley gets out of my sleepin' room," she stated.

"Well, I'm not getting out of your sleeping room. My foot hurts too much to walk on it." And so stating, he eased himself into a large leather chair and maneuvered the matching stool so his sore foot might rest on it.

"Well, I declare," Maggie said, looking her disgust. Assured he meant what he said, she reached for her wrapper and, still beneath the covers, managed to don it and tie the cord around her middle. Only then did she throw back the bedclothes and get out of bed, slipping her feet into her soft-soled crochet slippers.

"Thank you, Maggie," I said.

"Miss Betty, do you mind if I ask why I have to get everyone down here?"

"Yes, Maggie. But I have a reason. Please obey me."

"Yes, Miss." Stifling a yawn, she shuffled from the room.

Uncle Elijah rested his cane across the arms of the chair, propped his arms on them and regarded me thoughtfully. "Mind if *I* ask, my dear?"

"You'll know in due time," I said. "Just now, I want to know what you're doing downstairs."

His sigh was one of quiet resignation. "If you must know, I was hungry."

"So that's why your foot isn't getting better," I scolded. "You're cheating."

"I am indeed," he said. "I'm well on and the older one gets, the fewer the pleasures. I'm grateful my palate still relishes food. It's my greatest pleasure and fortunately my figure still gives no evidence I indulge myself."

"I don't know what Aunt Liz will say."

"I hope you won't tell her," he replied, for the first time looking worried.

"I shan't. But she's no more a fool than you, and is not easily fooled."

He regarded me thoughtfully. "Please tell me why you're having Maggie awaken the household."

"You'll know in due time," I said.

He worried his earlobe with his thumb and forefinger. "I was just thinking—if you'd called for help, it would be a good excuse for my being down here."

I might have smiled except that I was still upset by what I'd discovered in my bedroom. "You may say anything you wish. Though I'll not abet you in a lie, I'll not betray you either."

"Thank you, my dear. That's all I ask."

"I'd like to know why you think I'd have any reason to call for help," I said.

"When you asked or the envelope and I turned around, you looked as if you'd seen a ghost."

My smile was doubtful. "You could tell that, even in candlelight?"

"Maybe it was your tone of voice."

"If you detected anything in my voice, it was annoyance that you'd invaded the privacy of the room Maggie uses for sleeping."

He waved a hand in deprecation. "Now who'd even give that battle-ax a second look?"

"Don't let her hear you say that. At least, not until your foot's better and you can move faster than she."

There wasn't time for further talk because Maggie entered the room, followed by the others. She glared at Uncle Elijah, then walked over to stand by my chair, as if daring them to lay a hand on me.

Aunt Liz was the first to speak. "Elijah, how did you get down here?"

"I heard Betty's cry for help," he said, with a solemn shake of his head. "I don't know how I made it, but I did."

Maggie looked flabbergasted. "If Miss Betty called for help, I'da heard her."

"You were snoring so loud when I came in here, you'd deafen yourself," he retorted.

"That still gave you no call to come in here," she exclaimed contentiously. "And besides, I don't believe you."

"Frankly, Maggie Morfit, I don't give a damn whether you do or not," he replied, not even looking her way.

"Elijah," Aunt Liz exclaimed, "don't dare utter another blasphemous word in my presence or that of my niece. As for you," she pointed a finger at Maggie, "what do you mean by insinuating my husband is a liar?"

"I heard Miss Betty ask him what he was doing down here," Maggie retorted.

"I came down because I heard her scream," Uncle

Elijah replied, undaunted by her angry glare of disbelief.

Rena said, "Would you mind telling us why we were awakened out of a sound sleep?"

"I hope it was for a better reason than to hear Elijah and Maggie squabbling," Lew said, rubbing sleep from his eyes.

"It was," I said. "Will you go in my room, Lew? There's a garment on my bed. Bring it out, please."

He looked at me as if I'd lost my mind. "I came all the way down here to play errand boy? Can't Maggie do it?"

I nodded. "She could. Please do so, Maggie."

"I'll not leave your side, Miss. I don't trust a one of them."

"Please, Maggie, I felt quite safe with them. Go in my room and get the dress that's on the bed."

Lew relented with a smile. "I'm sorry. I'll go."

And he did. The rest of us remained silent, awaiting his return. After a few moments, he called out, "The only thing on your bed is the bedclothes."

"There's a dress on it," I called. "A dress of mine. It's a pale blue taffeta with rows of tiny pink bows around the deep hem of the skirt."

There was another few moments of silence, then he called, "I'm sorry. I can't find it."

"Take me in there, Maggie," I said.

She did, with the others following. There was no sign of the dress. "Please look under the bed," I addressed Lew.

"I already did, but I'll look again." And he got down on his hands and knees with the lamp, moving it the length of the bed. "There's nothing here. Not even a clump of dust, thanks to Lorette's eagle eye."

Aunt Liz said, "Maybe you dreamed it, my dear."

"I did not dream it," I said firmly. "It was hanging in front of that open window."

Maggie said, "That window wasn't opened when I left the room. I know because it was raining. It shouldn't be open now. It's damp in here."

"I know," I said. "It was the breeze blowing on my face that awakened me."

"I'll close it," Maggie said.

"Did you close the door between our rooms?" I asked.

"No, Miss. You know I always leave it open. I closed your bedroom window though."

"See if the dress could be outside the window," I said, knowing I must sound foolish.

Uncle Elijah apparently thought so too. "You don't suppose it sprouted wings and flew out, do you, dear?"

I looked around at him. He was standing in the doorway, but using the doorjamb as a support.

"No, Uncle. I think someone wanted to frighten me."

"In heaven's name, why, child?" Aunt Liz exclaimed.

"I don't know," I said. "I had no idea that dress was still around. It shouldn't be. It's a gory mess."

Uncle Elijah said, "How did you get in the chair?" As soon as he'd spoken, he knew he'd committed a *faux pas*.

Lew addressed Uncle Elijah, barely suppressing a smile. "I thought you must have helped her. After all, you said you heard her call for help."

Uncle Elijah regarded him scornfully. "I did. But she was in the chair by the time I got down. I don't move fast, you know."

Aunt Liz said tartly, "You're not supposed to be down here at all, you know."

"I know, but when I hear a lady cry for help, I'll come if I have to crawl. Particularly when the lady happens to be our niece."

Aunt Liz didn't look convinced. Neither did Rena or Lew and I couldn't blame them.

"Then I take it none of you know how my dress got in my room," I said, sorry now I'd roused them from their sleep.

"If it ever was here," Rena said, plainly piqued. Nor could I blame her.

"It was," I said quietly. "But I'm sorry I disturbed you. Good night."

"More like good morning," Aunt Liz said, softening her words with a smile. "Maggie, get her under the covers. She'll catch her death."

"I will, ma'am, as soon as you all leave. And I'd like to get back in my bed, provided the room is empty." Her glance, shifting to Uncle Elijah, was openly hostile. "It will be, you old harridan," Uncle Elijah roared.

"Behave yourself, Elijah," Aunt Liz exclaimed.

"It's all right, Ma'am," Maggie said, regarding him contemptuously. "I got no respect for a man who lies—or who sneaks food from the kitchen."

It took a few moments for Aunt Liz to recover her composure. "So *that's* what he was doing down here."

"That's what he was doing," Maggie retorted. "And it ain't the first time."

Uncle Elijah's belligerence quickly abated and he looked like a little boy who'd been caught with his hand in the cookie jar.

Aunt Liz's arm extended and she pointed a finger

in the direction of the hall. "Upstairs, Elijah Pauley, and don't you dare set foot out of your room until Dr. Jeffrey Egan gives you permission."

"Oh, come now, Liz, you know . . ."

"Silence!" she shouted, her voice as resonant as his. "Upstairs, I said."

He turned and hobbled through the den. Rena and Lew, looking amused, followed. Aunt Liz bent and kissed my cheek. "Try not to have any more nightmares, dear," she said.

"No, auntie," I said, repressing a sigh. Not one of them believed me, nor could I blame them. But I wondered what happened to the gown. Certainly, it didn't disintegrate, nor did it sprout wings to fly out the window."

When Maggie and I were alone, I said, "Before you close the window, will you see if someone might have tossed the dress out the window?"

She regarded me as if I were bereft of my senses. "You mean there really was a dress in here?"

"There really was, Maggie."

"And you think Mr. Lew threw it out the window?"

"I don't know what happened to it," I said, no longer able to keep the misery out of my voice.

"Miss," her hand rested awkwardly on my shoulder in what was meant to be a comforting gesture, "I don't want to upset you, but it could have been you dreamed it."

"It could have been," I said, too frustrated to indulge in further argument.

She wheeled me over to the bed and started to lift me from the chair.

"I got in this chair myself, Maggie. Let me see if I can get back in bed."

"I wouldn't if I were you, Miss. You look pretty peaked."

"Nevertheless, I must try."

And I did, nearly falling to the floor in my efforts.

"No more, Miss, please. Dr. Egan would be angry if you fell with me by your side."

I nodded. "I really need you, Maggie. I don't know how I did it. A fluke perhaps."

"I'll take off your negligee once you're in bed."

"No, I'll keep it on. I'm cold."

"As you wish." She settled me on my pillows, covered me well, put out my lamplight and left the room, leaving the door all the way open this time.

Alone in the darkness, I wished mightily for Jeffrey's presence. I knew I needed him. And, for the first time, I forgot my helplessness. I wanted him by my side to comfort me—to tell me he believed I'd seen and held the dress I'd been wearing on that awful day when my parents died through my carelessness. I stirred restlessly and the crackle of paper in my negligee pocket reminded me of the envelope I'd thrust into it. I wondered if Uncle Elijah knew of its contents, or if it was plain coincidence that had caused him to take that book down, thus loosening the envelope from its place of concealment. I wanted mightily to light the lamp and examine its contents. I hadn't even glanced at it when Uncle Elijah handed it to me. But it would keep until morning. I closed my eyes. My exertions had left me spent, but not so much so I started to wonder if someone in this house wished me ill.

THIRTEEN

It was a relief to awaken to bright sunshine, for the memory of the night before flooded through my mind. I wondered what had become of the blood-stained dress. I heard no sounds of Maggie stirring and decided she was still breakfasting. I turned and again became aware of the crackle of paper in my negligee pocket. I took out the envelope. It was a letter addressed to Papa. I was just about to remove the contents when I heard Maggie's voice mingled with Lorette's in the room beyond. I opened the drawer of the bedside table and slipped the envelope in it, then settled back on my pillows.

A moment later she entered the room and came directly to my bedside. "How are you this morning, Miss?"

"Well-rested," I said with a smile. "I hope the night's interruption didn't tire you."

"Indeed not," she said. "I'd still like to know though what your uncle was doing in my sleeping room."

I managed not to smile at her reference to the den as her sleeping room. Of course, that's exactly what it was, but her overwhelming indignation was amusing, though I too was curious to know Uncle Elijah's reason for having to select a book here when a large section of one wall in the suite they occupied was recessed and shelved for books.

To assuage her indignation, I said, "He's an avid reader and I suppose there was a particular book he wanted in here."

"Then why didn't he take it?" she asked. "He left it on the table."

"I suppose because I startled him and he forgot it," I said. "I called to you, Maggie, but I couldn't waken you."

"That's because the door I left open was closed, Miss," she said.

"And the window you closed was opened," I said remindfully.

"Who could have done it, I wonder," she said ruminatively.

"The same person who hung my gown on the window latch," I said. "I didn't even know that dress was still around. Certainly, it shouldn't be. It's torn and soiled with dirt and blood. The very sight of it made me cringe."

"It brought it all back to you," she said knowingly.

"It did, Maggie."

"Don't dwell on it, Miss. Would you like breakfast in here or the dining room?"

"In here, please," I said, thinking of the envelope in the drawer. I didn't wish to leave the room until I'd examined its contents. She got me into the chair and wheeled me into the bathroom. The routine of my morning ablutions was already established, and made easy by her capable ministrations.

She helped me back into my negligee and wheeled me into the bedroom. There, she tucked a cashmere afghan about my knees and a light paisley wool shawl about my shoulders.

"I'll get your breakfast now, Miss." She started from the room, but paused in the doorway. "Oh, Miss, there's a sick friend of mine in the village. Reggie brought me the message. Would you let me have the afternoon off to pay her a visit?"

"Certainly." The fates seemed to favor me. I was delighted she'd not be around, for I wished to talk with Jeffrey regarding the incident of the dress.

"I don't like to leave you after the fright you had last night," she went on. "But my friend needs a little care and I can give it to her."

"That's kind of you, Maggie," I said. "Why not take the entire day off?"

"It wouldn't be fair to you, Miss," she replied, though her eyes brightened at the suggestion.

"Nonsense," I replied. "There's Aunt Liz and Lorette to help me should I need anything."

"And the good doctor will stop by, I'm sure."

"If he has time. Neither Uncle Elijah nor I are in any urgent need of care."

"Your uncle I have no use for after last night—if you'll pardon my saying so, Miss."

"Don't be too harsh on him," I urged. "He's an older man and has few pleasures. I'm sure he wouldn't have harmed you."

"It ain't that. I'm strong and can take care of myself. It's that my pride was hurt. I like my privacy, especially in my sleepin' room."

"You're entitled to it, and I'll give orders that, from now on, no one is to set foot in your sleeping room, without first knocking and obtaining permission from you."

She gave a satisfied nod and looked quite mollified. "I'll appreciate it, Miss."

After she left, I eyed the drawer, but resisted temptation. Instead, I wheeled the chair to my clothes closet and opened the door. Enough light slipped into the windowless room to reveal the contents of my wardrobe. I scanned each dress carefully, opened my cloaks and capes to make certain the bedraggled gown wasn't concealed beneath any of them. I was still in there when she returned with my tray.

"Where are you, Miss?" she called out, momentarily startled at no sign of me.

"In the closet," I called, backing my chair out, for there wasn't enough width to turn around without getting entangled in my garments. I made no mention of my real reason for going in there, saying, "I was trying to decide what to wear today."

"And what will it be?" Maggie spoke as she placed my breakfast on the table before the window.

"The light blue woolen frock with the ruffled collar and cuffs. It's rather cool after the rain."

"It is," she agreed. "And it's pretty on you. Matches the blue of your eyes."

I poured cream on the dish of peaches which were at their peak of ripeness. They tasted as delicious as they looked, for they were tender and juicy. The bacon was crisp and the eggs fried exactly as I wanted them. The coffee was strong and, though I added no sugar, I was generous with the cream. Gildy saw to it I was getting the proper nourishment. But I knew that, if I continued to eat in this fashion, I'd have to work harder to get out of this chair.

Maggie brought out my tray of dishes, cleared of all food, and came back with word that Gildy was pleased. Once I was dressed, I insisted she go out to the stable and inform Chuck he was to take her to the village. She hung up my nightdress and negligee first and, though it seemed to me she remained in the closet longer than necessary, it could have been due to the fact that, after last night, I was allowing seeds of suspicion to be planted in my mind. I couldn't help but wonder though if she checked the pocket of my negligée to see if the letter still reposed there. I was pleased I'd had enough presence of mind to slip it in the bedside table drawer.

Maggie excused herself then, thanking me once again. I told her I would remain in my room for awhile and look out the window. I had a lovely view of the distant mountains, still partially mist-shrouded. I'd also have a view of the drive and I'd know when she left. I waved to her as she headed for the stable to pass on my order to Chuck and again when she returned to the house. She kept her clothes in her upstairs room and so had to go there to change out of her uniform.

Aunt Liz came in for a few minutes to tell me Uncle Elijah seemed none the worse for sneaking food from the kitchen and she wished the good doctor would allow him to resume his normal activity. I couldn't tell her that Jeffrey was more concerned about Uncle Elijah's heart than his attack of gout which he considered mild. I was greatly concerned lest his exertions of ascending the stairs might have placed undue strain on it. I would speak to Jeffrey when he came, for it was only fair he know of Uncle Elijah's disobedience. Perhaps, I thought, Jeffrey suspected. He was very astute. I was impatient to see him, but I also wanted to see Harley and I asked Aunt Liz if she'd request Lew to go to the quarry and relay that message to Harley. She said she would do so at once.

It wasn't more than fifteen minutes later that I waved a farewell to Maggie. She waved back energetically, then settled back in the carriage, assuming a dignified posture. She was a proud person and I knew she'd thoroughly enjoy her ride to the village.

I wheeled my chair over to the bedroom table, opened the drawer and took out the envelope. It was a business letter from a gentleman named Canfield. He was in charge of the office Papa maintained in Boston. The letter was dated three days prior to Papa's death. The missive itself seemed quite ordinary, stating that a shipment of white marble meant for the new buildings beginning to go higher and higher in New York City had not arrived and a tentative delivery date was being asked for. But there was a postscript I found highly intriguing. It was brief and read: *Your request for experienced, trustworthy man now being explored. Will inform you promptly when I find a replacement.*

The request for a trustworthy man was, indeed, puzzling. Immediately three names came to mind—Harley, Reggie and Dudley. I'd always considered them completely honest and believed Papa was of the same opinion. Yet this letter placed a nagging doubt in my mind. I folded it and replaced it in the envelope. Handicapped as I was, I had no place to hide it. So far as I knew, the house did not contain a metal strongbox. I didn't know whether or not the office at the quarry did. But even so, I wanted no one, either at the quarry or the house, to see this letter. I slipped it into my skirt pocket for want of a better place.

I was saddened that I felt it necessary to include the occupants of the house in the category of those not to be trusted, but after last night, I felt I could trust no one here, with the possible exception of Lorette and Maggie. I doubted the latter had even known of the existence of the dress. One thing I did know—no one I'd summoned last night believed anyone had hung the frock on the casement window. At least, if any member of the group had been pretending ignorance, they gave an excellent performance.

I went through the papers and correspondence in Papa's desk, but there was nothing more of a suspicious nature. I was impatient for Jeffrey to arrive and fearful some emergency might prevent him from coming. I regarded the shelves of books in the library, wondering if, concealed among them, there might be more letters which might name the person whom Papa had distrusted. I did inspect the books on the first shelf which were within my reach, but without success.

After our noonday meal, I retired to my chamber and massaged my leg muscles. I was diligent about it, though it wasn't always easy. However, today Rena and Lew took one carriage to town.

Chuck had returned after bringing Maggie to her destination, for Aunt Liz visited Mrs. Seaver faithfully each afternoon. She refused pointblank to go with Lew, stating they might wish to return before she was ready to leave and she thoroughly enjoyed her afternoons with Mrs. Seaver.

Before Aunt Liz left, she came in with a note

from Harley in which he begged my indulgence, asking if he might postpone his visit to the Castle until evening because of a heavy work schedule at the quarry. She told me one of the workers was waiting for my reply. I penned a brief note, stating the evening would be quite satisfactory and to come for supper if he wished.

And so, except for Uncle Elijah, confined to his quarters upstairs, the Castle was deserted, for both Gildy and Lorette had accompanied Aunt Liz to the village. Lorette, to attend a quilting bee and Gildy to place a large order of groceries at the general store. Mama had always let her make the purchases and I saw no reason to change it.

And so I was on the porch when Jeffrey came down the drive. He called out a "Whoa" to the animal, jumped down from the buggy and slipped the reins loosely through a ring held by a metal figure which sat near the stairs.

"You know," he said, regarding me carefully, "for the first time, you look genuinely glad to see me."

Though I smiled, I felt color flush my face. "You may be right. I suddenly realized how important and how necessary you are to me."

"God bless you for saying it." He took both my hands, raised them to his lips, then said, "Let's seek out our favorite spot."

"First, please go up and pay Uncle Elijah a visit," I said. "He's alone. And, in confidence, I must tell you he comes downstairs and secretly raids the pantry."

Jeffrey didn't look the least bit surprised. "I suspected that. But, as I told you, my main reason for keeping him confined is that I don't like him using the stairs because of his heart."

"In that case, I must learn to walk so he may have the room I'm using," I said. "I'll await you here."

"I shan't be long," he promised.

"Do take a little time with him," I urged. "He's lonely and, though he's slowed down physically, mentally he's very sharp. Also, he's a bit of an extrovert and is most happy when he has an audience."

Jeff said, "No wonder I love you," and squeezed my hands. He went inside then and I heard his rapid steps echo through the vast hall as he ascended the marble stairs.

I sat there waiting for him, quite unaware of the coolness generated by the marble portico, for I felt warmed by his love. I knew now what it was like to relish the devotion of a good man. How comforting and safe one felt. And how necessary love was for one's growth and well-being. How often I'd heard the saying, love makes the world go round. Yet, up until now, I'd taken it for granted. I wouldn't from now on, for I'd never felt so blessed.

It took my fright of the night before to make me realize how much I needed Jeffrey. I'd not be a burden to him, I told myself. I'd be interested in his work and his patients and, even though my legs would never support my body, I had a whole mind and I'd develop it. I'd always loved reading, though I was quite ignorant regarding the medical field. Now I'd study it. The world of healing the ill was a strange one to me, but I'd read everything available so I could converse intelligently on the subject with my beloved. I knew now what Dr. Beardsley had meant when he told me I must stop thinking constantly of myself. I was hurt and indignant when he'd told me I was filled with self-pity. Angered when Jeffrey had supported that statement, but they'd spoken the truth. And how well aware I now was of it. I felt filled with such a feeling of exhilaration I wanted to get out of the chair, go down the steps and run, run, run.

Then I shuddered, for that is what I'd been doing when I tripped over the wire which set off the explosive of dynamite. I still couldn't rid myself of the feeling of guilt. Yet, whereas before, I'd assured myself I'd never walk again, and felt it was my punishment, now I had an overwhelming desire to stand and move about on my own. I had no assurance I could, but I'd not give up until I heard the words pass Jeffrey's lips that I must live out my life in a wheelchair.

I don't know how long he was gone, for I was content, knowing he was near and would be with me soon. When he finally came down, he reported that Uncle Elijah seemed none the worse for his night's adventure.

"He also told me you had a fright," Jeff said, loosening the brake of the chair and guiding it carefully down the steps. He paused at the buggy and took from it a pair of crutches. "I think it's about time you started working with these."

"Do you think it's possible?" I exclaimed. The thought of using crutches had never occurred to me.

"Not only possible, but necessary. It's opportune that no one is about today so we can keep it a secret for awhile."

"Yes," I said. "I think it would be safer for me if we did."

"Your uncle didn't go into detail about you because he was more concerned with making excuses for himself," Jeff chuckled. "Finally, he said he was damned if he'd apologize for sneaking food. It was the only pleasure left to him. So I told him to go ahead and enjoy himself, provided he remained upstairs for a few more days."

"I'm glad," I said. "He does enjoy good food and Gildy is an excellent cook and likes to see her efforts rewarded by having dishes come back empty."

I insisted on placing the crutches across the arms of the chair and Jeffrey headed directly for the path, guiding the chair skillfully along the still-damp ground. However, the area we favored was well-sheltered and I doubted it would hinder my efforts to walk or to learn how to use the crutches.

Once we arrived at the spot, he insisted I tell him first what had happened. I did and he listened soberly. Even when I'd completed my story, he made no comment and so I handed him the letter which had been received by Papa only two days before his untimely death.

After Jeffrey read it, he asked, "Do you have any idea who the untrustworthy employee was or is?"

"Not the slightest. I know it couldn't be a member of the family, for neither my aunt and uncle nor Cousin Lew and his wife, were here. Nor were they ever employed in any capacity with the quarry."

"It obviously referred to someone holding an important position," Jeffrey mused. "Which means either Harley or Reggie."

"Or Dudley," I said. "Besides bookkeeping, he handles the payroll."

"Does anyone else know about this letter or its

contents?"

"I have no idea," I said. "I hope not."

"So do I," he said. "Someone's trying to frighten you, you know."

I nodded. "But what happened to the dress?"

"Someone could have come in through that open window while you were in the den and got it out of there. Or it could have been hidden in the room somewhere and retrieved after you went back to sleep."

"Or thrown out the window."

"That too," he admitted.

"I checked my closet this morning," I said. "Lew looked under the bed last night at my suggestion, to see if it might have fallen there. He said there wasn't a sign of it."

"What awakened you?" Jeffrey asked.

"The cool, rain-scented breeze," I said. "Maggie closed the window before she left the room. And she always leaves the door connecting the library and my bedroom ajar. It was tightly closed."

"Did you check the floor of your room to see if it was muddied by footprints?"

"No," I admitted. "But I'm sure I'd have noticed any such thing this morning. As I told you, I checked my closet to see if the gown might have been concealed behind dresses or beneath a mantle. It wasn't there."

"Was anyone else in the room before you returned to it?"

"Only Lew. I asked him to get the dress. He was annoyed at first at the thought of having been awakened to come down and play errand boy. Then I asked Maggie to do it. She refused to leave my side, saying she didn't trust any of them. She was miffed anyway at Uncle Elijah for entering her sleeping room, as she refers to the den. I couldn't really blame her."

Jeffrey smiled. "Your uncle told me about that."

"Indignantly, I'm sure."

"Quite," Jeffrey agreed. "I fear he doesn't consider Maggie a very comely female. I'm afraid I must agree with him that her fears were needless."

"She wasn't fearful," I told Jeffrey. "It was her dignity which had been impugned."

"Despite the humorous side, this thing is very serious. I'm concerned for your safety."

"Then you believe I saw the dress hanging from the window latch," I said.

"Certainly. Didn't the others?"

"No. Not one of them. They thought I had a nightmare. It was as bad as if I had. But it wasn't, for I wheeled my chair over to the window, sending it against the wall. The dress slipped from the latch and fell into my lap. When I went back to the light and saw what it was, I was horrified and threw it on the bed. It was in horrible condition, but it carried a strong scent of lavender. Mama's favorite fragrance and mine, I might add."

His brow furrowed thoughtfully. "Did it ever occur to you that you were, in no way, responsible for the death of your parents?"

"No," I replied promptly.

"Suppose the person learned your father suspected him. Suppose he'd taken a great deal of money from the firm and dared not risk discovery."

"What you're saying is that Mama and Papa were murdered."

"That's exactly what I'm saying."

"It was I who tripped over the wire," I said remindfully.

"Either of your parents might have done so. You told me your father walked here daily, often pointing out various points of interest regarding the quarry, to you and your mother."

"True," I said, appalled by the idea that had never once occurred to me. And why should it, I thought. I believed everyone held Papa in the highest respect.

"Therefore," Jeffrey went on, "this person, knowing that, realized the best place to do away with your father would be here. No suspicion would be diverted to the killer, for it would be assumed to have been an accident."

I nodded and Jeffrey continued. "That's exactly what everyone thought. There was just one flaw in that macabre plan. You didn't die. With you alive, there was still danger of his being found out. So long as you were in the hospital, the murderer was relatively safe for, obviously, your father mentioned no names when he wrote to," Jeffrey tapped the letter, "this Mr. Canfield asking for a trustworthy replacement. But just as obviously, the murderer was aware of your father's suspicions regarding him."

"And now that I'm back, that person fears me," I said.

"And apparently wants to cast suspicion on your sanity. Particularly since the dynamite blast didn't kill you."

"You mean, the day Maggie and I were out," I exclaimed.

"I do. Are you sure no one suggested you go to the spot which overlooked the quarry?"

"Quite sure," I said. "Maggie and I had been talking—or rather she had been trying to talk me out of the feeling of guilt I had regarding my parents."

"Can you recall the conversation?"

"Not precisely," I said.

"Try," he urged.

I thought a moment. "She told me she thought she'd never get over her Joseph's death, but she finally did. I reminded her that she had nothing to do with the accident that took his life. She admitted that."

Jeffrey squatted before me. "But how did you happen to go to that particular area where the dynamite explosion occurred?"

"I don't know," I exclaimed, irritated by the intenseness of his voice.

"Think, Betty. You must. You must remember. It's important."

"I—I said to her, 'I suppose I can't avoid the spot the rest of my life.' She agreed."

"Did you tell her to take you there?" he prodded. "Did *you* tell *her* or was it *her* suggestion?"

My eyes widened in astonishment.

"What is it?" he asked.

"Maggie." I spoke her name slowly, in shocked remembrance.

"What about her?" He cupped my face between his hands. "Tell me, my darling."

"It was her suggestion," I said slowly. "I remember now. She thought I would like to see the quarry. I told her I wouldn't, as I didn't think I could ever go to that spot again. Then I felt ashamed—as if I were a coward and stated I supposed I couldn't avoid the spot forever. I remember now her exact reply."

"Tell me," he prompted.

"She said, 'That's for sure, Miss.'"

Jeffrey released my face and sat back on his haunches. "Maggie," he said reflectively. "What would be her motive and who told her to do that?"

"I don't know," I said.

"Nor do I, but her motive is simple enough. Revenge for her husband's death."

"You mean that's why she came to the Castle and asked permission to tend me—without pay? She wasn't satisfied by what happened to my parents?"

"Apparently not."

"Do you suppose it was her idea to come here and serve me without pay or someone else's?"

"Someone else's," he replied promptly. "She isn't smart enough to figure out those things. I imagine she's been promised a tidy sum of money."

"I thought of something else," I said. "Just before the explosion, she glanced at her watch."

"She was ordered to bring you there. You were to be killed. And you almost were."

"But she did catch the chair," I said remindfully.

"Perhaps to allay suspicion from herself," he replied. "It may be she was tilting the chair so you'd tumble out. Which you did. It was your own presence of mind which saved you."

"Not completely," I said. "She caught my wrist and held on."

"Again, perhaps because she feared you might not die and would suspect it was not an accident."

"But it's still supposition."

"I'll grant that, but she'll bear watching."

"I asked her last night after everyone left my room if she would look out the window and see if my dress might be lying on the ground. She said it wasn't. I don't know what made me do that, except I knew it had to be someplace. The only other person in the room was Lew and he certainly couldn't have concealed it on his person."

"He could have thrown it out the window," Jeffrey said.

"He has no motive," I said. "I can't believe he put it in there. I don't believe anyone except Lorette saw that dress. I had no idea it had been kept."

"Do you trust Lorette?"

"Implicitly."

"Ask her what she knows about the dress when no one else is around."

"I will."

"And now, my love, I have one more question. Then we'll start the therapy."

"What is it?"

"When did you decide to accept my love?"

"Last night," I said, "after no one believed me. I felt very alone and frightened and after I was back in my bed again, I wished with all my heart you were close so I could talk with you. I knew you'd believe me. I needed your love and comfort and I realized I'd never allow myself to be a burden to you, even though my legs might never support me."

His eyes were warm with the love he bore me, but his voice was a quiet command as he said, "Tell me you love me."

"I love you, my darling Jeffrey. I shall always love you from this day on until I take my last breath."

"May that be many years hence, for we are both young and have much living to do." With that, he raised me to my feet and held me to him. This time, my arms went around his neck and I raised my face for his kiss. We held the embrace and I thought my heart would burst with the ecstasy of a love I no longer denied.

Then he released me. I was trembling with emotion, and the tremor in his voice when he murmured an endearment, revealed he'd been deeply affected also. But the wonder was, I was standing alone, unsupported and steadily. He stepped back beyond my reach and extended his arms for me to come to him. When I extended mine to reach for his hands, he moved back still further. Strengthened by his love, I could do no more but go to him. Cautiously, I raised a foot, moved it a scant two inches and set it on the ground again. I did the same with the other. I repeated it twice more before I fell into his arms. Again he drew me close and murmured endearments and kissed my eyelids, the tips of my ears and the hollow of my throat. I was faint with delight. Then he picked me up and settled me in the chair. He knew I needed to regain my senses before I could attempt the crutches. And we sat there for an hour. I insisted he tell me about himself and his boyhood. He smiled tolerantly, but seemed hesitant to do so. However, all I had to do was ask him a few leading questions and, from then on, it was easy.

Finally he said, "Why is it when a woman falls in love with a man, one of the first things she wants to know is everything about his boyhood? It seems so irrelevant."

I laughed. "I suppose its' because she's such a possessive creature."

"So that's it." His laughter intermingled with mine. It really wasn't that humorous, except to us. "Do you feel up to trying the crutches?"

"I feel so wonderful I think I could sprout wings and fly."

"Not that," he said. "You might get away from me. I had too hard a time convincing you you should love me."

Our levity stopped then, for he had me on my feet and had the crutches under my arms. I was awkward, but eager, perhaps too eager because he had to caution me to exercise more care. But I settled down and managed to master the use of them, not easily, but in time I would do so.

"That's enough for today," Jeffrey said. "You know, I was going to suggest we let the others know you have been making progress and will, I believe, one day walk in a perfectly normal manner. Now I don't believe we should reveal that."

"Nor I," I said. "I'm keeping Maggie. In the first place, we lack proof she's engaged in complicity of any kind. In the second place, I might learn something from her."

"Be careful," he cautioned. "She may not be very bright, but she could be sly. We must do nothing to force the murderer's hand. I'm going to put the crutches in the mausoleum. I doubt anyone would have a reason for coming there."

I nodded agreement. He brought me back then, cautioning me to do my best to act as if nothing had changed. Also, not to refer to the dress again except to question Lorette, provided I could trust her. I still felt certain I could and so stated. I also asked him to keep the letter lest it be stolen.

He wheeled me back to the Castle then, but just before we left, he regarded the angel atop the front of the mausoleum. "You know," he said, studying it carefully, "it somehow looks different to me."

"I don't see any difference," I said. "Though I dislike it placed on top as much as ever."

"So do I. Why don't you have it moved?"

"I will." I said impulsively. "I'll speak to Harley about it."

Jeffrey leaned forward and spoke in my ear. "Did you know that rumor in the village has it that you and he . . . ?"

"I know all about it," I said, interrupting him. "There's no truth in it. You know Harley's reputation with the ladies as well as I. He could never be faithful to one. The only gentleman I'm interested in has wheeled me off the path and if he doesn't tend to his chores, I'm going to collide with one of those marble columns."

"Forgive me, my dear," he said, chuckling and getting the chair back on the path. "I just needed reassurance."

"You have it," I said.

I raised my hand up to his. Our fingers entwined and that was the way we returned to the Castle. A little awkward for him, but heavenly for me.

FOURTEEN

Jeffrey had been gone only a short while when Rena and Lew returned from the village. They visited me in the den for a while, each hoping I felt better after my nightmare.

I went along with it, apologizing and agreeing the nightmare had seemed so real I actually believed it had happened. I didn't bother to remind them Maggie had stated, in their presence, that she'd closed my bedroom window against the rain, or that she'd left the door to our adjoining rooms open.

They took their leave then and I wheeled myself over to the window. No sooner had I done so than I saw the others returning. I waved a greeting to them and moved into the hall to bid them welcome.

They each looked stimulated by their little expedition and I was glad they'd gone and returned in a group. Their faces were animated and their eyes sparkled with the excitement of their day. Gildy handed me the list of items she'd purchased along with the amount they cost.

"That goes into the file your papa kept in the den on the third shelf behind his desk," Lorette informed me.

"Please come in and get it for me, Lorette," I said.

She did so willingly and it gave me an opportunity

to talk with her. I told her briefly about the incident of the dress. Her eyes in her thin face widened in shocked amazement.

"I hope you believe me," I said.

"I've never known of you to lie, Miss, even as a child," she said. "That was a horrible thing to have happen."

"It was and more so, since the dress disappeared seemingly into thin air."

"But where could it have gone?" she asked.

"I don't know," I said. "What I wished to ask you, more than anything, was—did you know the dress had been kept?"

"No, Miss. I'm sure it wasn't kept in this house. I know every garment that hangs in the closet and I know what's stored in the attic."

"But who would have wanted to keep such a bedraggled thing?"

Her head moved wonderingly from side to side. "I got no idea, Miss. But it's sure scary."

I had to agree. "Please don't say anything about it to the others. I don't think they believe me, but truly, the dress was in my room."

"I believe you, Miss," she said. "And I promise not to say a word."

I smiled my thanks. "Now, Lorette, will you please hand me down the proper file?"

She did so. I placed the list in it after making a note of the amount due the general store. I would make out a check later. She replaced the file, excused herself and left the room.

Aunt Liz came in then. "Maggie asks to be excused a little longer. She's a bit fatigued. Too much gadding about, I guess."

"She wasn't gadding, Aunt Liz," I said, chiding her gently. "She was caring for a sick friend."

She gave me an arch look. "I beg to differ. Mrs. Seaver and I sit in her front room by the windows, as you know. We saw Maggie and Reggie's wife go into the ice cream parlor. They were there easily two hours and if you'll also pardon my saying so, Maggie burped all the way home so I guess she had her fill of ice cream bought, I'm sure, by Mrs. Mandaray. But then," she added, "I think Maggie's entitled to it, considering."

"What do you mean?" I asked.

"Will you ever forget the supper the night Mrs. Mandaray was here?" Aunt Liz asked indignantly. "She chattered like a magpie. No one else got a word in edgewise."

I smiled. "I'd forgotten."

"I haven't," she declared. "Next time you invite her, I'll plead sick."

"How is Mrs. Seaver?" I asked, to change the subject.

"Just the same. But cheerful as ever."

"You know, being in her presence and observing her marvelous disposition was really what brought me to my senses. Though I can't walk, I have no pain, while her poor body is wracked with it."

"She suffers in silence," Aunt Liz said, her smile soft. "Did you know your papa visited Dudley every night for about a month before the—accident?"

"No!" I exclaimed, openly astounded.

"Well, he did. She told me John—of course she referred to your father as Mr. Bowen, not being the type to take liberties—came there and he and Dudley talked far into the night."

"About what?"

"How should I know?"

I gave her a knowing glance. "Didn't you ask?"

She colored with embarrassment. "All right, I did. But Mrs. Seaver said she had no idea. They talked in undertones."

"Dudley would know though." Without realizing it, I'd expressed the thought aloud.

"Good heavens, Betty, I hope you won't have him come here to ask what he and your papa talked about. Mrs. Seaver would be real put out with me and I wouldn't blame her."

"Nor would I, Aunt Liz. Be assured, I'll not betray your confidence."

"Thank you." She bent and kissed my cheek. "I'm very fond of Mrs. Seaver and I enjoy being with her so much."

"I'm sure she appreciates your company," I said.

She smiled. "She was very fond of your mama. She said Clarissa was always bringing her something. And she loves the shawl. She wears it, you know. And she told me to tell you that Dudley cherishes his pipe, particularly since he knew it was meant for your papa. Seems you talked with Dudley about getting your papa one and even asked what kind he'd like."

"So I did," I exclaimed. "I'd completely forgotten."

Aunt Liz started to go, then turned back. "You know she said something else. I thought it kind of strange."

I managed to keep my voice calm as I said, "Please tell me."

"She said Dudley told her your papa said he was going to see to it that neither she nor Dudley would ever be in want in case anything ever happened to him, meaning your papa, of course. And she said he meant it in case anything happened to Dudley. Did you know anything about that?"

"No," I replied. "But if she says Papa said that, I'm sure he did. Apparently he was killed before he could do anything about it. Thank you for telling me, Aunt Liz. I'll see to it they'll never be in need."

"Thank you, my dear," she said, looking gratified. "I knew you would. But please don't let either Dudley or his mother know I told you this. It would upset them both, I know."

"I'll wait a decent interval before doing it," I promised.

She nodded, satisfied. "Now I must go upstairs and see your uncle."

"Jeffrey said he's much better."

"So he was here again today," she said, regarding me thoughtfully. "What do you two find to talk about?"

I said, quite blandly, "His work. His interest in doctoring, plus his interest in the villagers. He's a very dedicated physician, you know."

She smiled. "I know. I also think he's very dedicated to a certain Betty Bowen."

"Oh, come now, Auntie. You're letting your imagination take over."

"Indeed I'm not. I've seen the way he looks at you. Frankly, I was hoping you'd encourage him. I'd like to plan a social for you—and invite all the villagers—but I can't unless you have an escort."

"Very well, Aunt Liz," I acquiesced. "You may plan the social and invite all the villagers. I'll ask the good doctor to be my escort."

"Oh, my dear, I'm so glad." She clapped her hands in glee. "I'll go right upstairs now and start making plans. May we really put on a show?"

"Make it as lavish as you wish," I told her.

She came back and bestowed another kiss on my brow. "I'm as happy for you as I am for me. This place needs laughter and gaiety once again. When Clarissa and John were alive, I loved being invited here, for laughter and happiness flowed through the marbled corridors like a spring breeze."

"I remember," I told her, "and it's about time it came back."

Maggie came in shortly after Aunt Liz left. I said, "I hope your friend wasn't too indisposed."

"There was nothing wrong with her," Maggie scoffed. "She gets frightened at the merest pain. Wouldn't even let me stay."

"What's her name?"

"No one you know, Miss. Only moved here since the accident that took your mama and papa."

"A pity you had to spend the day by yourself."

"I did no such thing," she replied spiritedly. "I paid Mrs. Mandaray a visit. The night she was here for supper, she told me to be sure to stop by the next time I was in the village. A lovely lady."

"Very," I agreed hypocritically.

"She took me to the ice cream parlor and I must say I had my fill, Miss. It was a real treat and Mrs. Mandaray paid for it."

"I'm glad you weren't alone."

"Indeed I wasn't. When I stopped to visit her, she showed me her clothes. Mrs. Adams makes all of them, you know."

"I didn't know," I replied, quite surprised, knowing Mrs. Adams charged a goodly fee for her services.

"Oh yes. Whenever your mama had a gown made, Mrs. Mandaray had Mrs. Adams copy it, but in another color, of course."

"Did Mama know it?"

Maggie's smile was conspiratorial. "I think not, Miss. Mrs. Mandaray wore them only when she went to Boston. She has lots of hats too. Stacks of hat boxes."

"I would enjoy seeing them," I said. "Reggie must be very generous with her."

"No more so than with himself. She showed me his closet, stuffed with dressing gowns, suits, even evening clothes. They go to Boston a lot, though she did say since you came back, they haven't been."

"I certainly had nothing to do with stopping them," I said.

She regarded me thoughtfully. "Did you mean that for sarcasm, Miss?"

"Indeed not, Maggie. I merely meant they shouldn't change their way of life just because I'm back at the Castle."

She nodded and I wondered if I'd convinced her. "Bowen's Castle," she mouthed the words carefully, letting them slide over her tongue slowly. "I used to look at it from the road, just aching to get inside and see what it looked like and here I am in it, taking care of the princess."

I stiffened. "Please don't call me that."

"I mean no offense, Miss," she said quickly.

"I'm sure you didn't," I replied, managing a smile. "But I'm not a princess. Merely a young lady and a rather helpless one. However, one no longer discouraged, for I'm determined to live a normal life, even if I never leave my wheelchair."

"That's the spirit, Miss," she said, with a firm nod of her head.

"Thank you, Maggie. Now will you please wheel me into my room? I'd like a nap before supper. Oh, one thing more. Will you tell my cousin I would like to see him?"

"Certainly, Miss. Right away."

And she was prompt. Lew came into my room quickly, closing the door behind him, shutting out my view of Maggie. I caught the look of surprise on her face, but I was pleased he had enough presence of mind to do it.

"Lew, will you go to the quarry and ask Dudley to please come here before he goes home?"

"Of course," he said. "I could use a little walk. Rena's nagging me about a trip to Europe. How does she think I could afford such a thing?"

"When does she wish to leave?" I asked.

"As soon as possible. Our fifth wedding anniversary is next month."

"A European trip shall be my anniversary present to you," I said.

"No, Betty, I wouldn't accept it. It's embarrassing enough now, living here on your bounty."

"I want you living here. With my handicap, I'd be too lonely without the sound of voices echoing through the corridors."

"I still refuse," he said. "I'll give Dudley your message." He started to leave, then turned abruptly, snapping his fingers as he did so. "I just thought of a way I could satisfy Rena and earn the voyage to Europe."

"Please tell me. I want you to go."

"Perhaps I could sell some marble while I'm there."

"Would you really be interested in that?"

"I truly would."

I was touched by his sincerity. "Splendid. We'll discuss it with Harley. I'm sure he'd have no objection."

I smiled reassurance. "If he does, I'll overrule him. I believe I'm in a position to do so."

He brightened. "You know, I believe you are."

He left the room with a light step and I caught a glimpse of him through the open door chucking Maggie under the chin. She slapped his hand away, favoring him with a look of disgust, then came in the room to help me into bed.

"He's as bad as your uncle," she said.

"He was only teasing you, Maggie," I told her.

"I ain't the type for foolishness, Miss. I demand respect."

"You're entitled to it. And I'll inform him he's not to do it again."

"Thank you, Miss. Is there anything you'd like?"

"Nothing, Maggie."

"Then I'll take a stroll about the grounds. I had too much ice cream and rich syrup. A walk will work it down a little."

"Run along. I'll have no need of you."

"Rest now, Miss."

Much to my amazement I did, slipping off into a deep sleep immediately. I was surprised when she wakened me, telling me if I didn't get up, I'd be late for the evening meal. I still felt tired, and realized my efforts with the crutches along with those few steps I'd taken today had exhausted me more than I realized, but I also felt highly gratified I'd made that small bit of progress.

"Did anyone come to the Castle while I was sleeping?"

"Not that I know of, Miss."

"You wouldn't know really, Maggie. You were out."

"True. Would you like me to find out?"

"No need. I'll question the others at the table."

And I did. Lew assured me he'd delivered the message to Dudley who said he'd come to the house directly from work. Yet the hour was seven and I knew the quarry shut down at six.

"Perhaps he forgot," Aunt Liz said when she learned my reason for asking.

"I hardly think Dudley is the type who'd forget," I replied. "I hope nothing's happened to him."

"What possibly could happen?" Aunt Liz queried. "He stays in the office with his books all the time, doesn't he?"

"That's where he was when I delivered your message," Lew said.

"Yes, he was," Rena said. "I went with Lew. And thanks, Betty, for your anniversary gift. Lew said he'd accept, provided he could try his efforts at selling marble over there."

"It won't be difficult," Lew said. "Harley told me the marble from this quarry is in great demand abroad, but your papa always gave preference to this country."

"And why not?" Aunt Liz demanded. "This country is still young and has a lot of building to do and those who are willing to take the risk of investing their money should be given the best to work with."

"Hear, hear," Lew exclaimed, though his smile

gave evidence of his agreement. "It's just that I'd like to do something to feel I was earning that trip."

"I'm sure there's enough marble in the quarry to serve any European clients that wish it," I told him.

"They want only the best," Lew said.

"We'll discuss it with Harley, but not tonight. I have other matters to talk about with him."

"Thanks, Betty," Lew said. He blew me a kiss across the table.

Maggie made a tsk-tsking sound of disdain. The rest of us exchanged knowing glances, but refrained from making any comment.

After dinner I asked Maggie to wheel me back to the den, stating I was expecting Harley. He hadn't come for dinner, but I was sure he wouldn't disappoint me. I would have been hurt by Dudley's nonappearance, were I not so disturbed by it. It was so unlike him. I only hoped Harley would come. If he didn't, I'd send Lew to the quarry, though making certain Chuck accompanied him.

But my fears regarding Harley were short-lived, for I was no sooner settled before the fireplace in the den than I heard Lorette greeting him. The next moment he came charging into the room.

"How beautiful you look," he exclaimed. "And how ashamed I am you had to summon me."

"What do you mean?" I asked, amused as always by his brash manner.

"I should stop by each day to wish you well," he replied, seating himself on a stool at my feet. "But we're very far behind in our work. Can't keep up with the orders."

"I understand, Harley," I said. "Just remember, I'm always pleased to see you whenever you can find the time to pay me a visit. I'm the one who's been remiss. I was going to work with you if you remember."

"And you would have," he stated, "were it not for that dynamite charge which was a terrible shock to you. I think you should stay away from the place for awhile."

"You may be right," I said. "It may just be I'm not cut out for that sort of thing, though I know Papa would have been pleased to know I took an interest in the quarry. Maybe one day I will."

"Whenever you're ready, you need only summon me. I'm your willing servant."

"Thank you, Harley."

He took out his pocket watch, opened its engraved cover and glanced at the time. "Was there something special you wanted of me?"

If he'd come this morning when I'd sent for him, I'd really have been at a loss as to how to broach the subject uppermost on my mind, but now I felt I could lead into it in a perfectly normal manner. I also sensed Harley was eager to be off, probably for an evening's pleasure with a ladyfriend.

"Lew and I talked briefly this afternoon about his being our European representative in regard to selling marble abroad," I said. "I gather he talked with you also."

Harley smiled. "A little. I met him and Rena just as they came out of the office. They visited Dudley."

"No," I corrected him. "They delivered a message to Dudley for me. They were to tell him to stop by the Castle before he left for home."

"I didn't know," he said. "Didn't he?"

"No," I replied.

"That's not like him," he said.

"My precise thought," I said. "I'm concerned."

"I don't think there's anything to be concerned about," he said. "Perhaps he had to get back to his mother and will be here later."

"If such was the case, I believe he would have told Lew," I said.

"Yes," he agreed.

"Was he still there when you left?"

"No. I didn't see him leave though. But then, I didn't see Reggie either."

"It could be he forgot," I said, "and I'm worrying needlessly."

"I think you are, Betty. But it's nice of you to show concern about your employees."

"After what happened to my parents, how can I help it?"

"That was an accident due to dynamite," he said. "The horror of it is, it was almost repeated when you came back from the hospital."

I managed a smile. "I survived it."

"Thank God for that."

"Harley, just what did happen at the time of the explosion which killed Mama and Papa?"

"What happened? Why—I wasn't there, Betty. I can't answer that except to tell you what I found immediately afterward."

"That might be of importance," I said.

"The whole area where your father and mother were standing had been prepared for dynamiting. The holes had been bored in from the cliff wall, not down through the ground, so there'd be no evidence of it having been done to anyone standing on top of the cliff. The wires led to a battery box and they were attached—that is, I suppose they must have been. The box was placed close by the edge of the cliff. The explosives man had orders to set off the charge right after the quarry closed for the day. It was going to start an avalanche and make a great deal of dust which wouldn't settle for hours. That's why the blast was delayed so the dust would have cleared by morning and the men could go to work."

"Did Papa know there was to be a blast that day?"

Harley answered promptly. "Certainly he knew, but before the charge was set off, we'd have made sure the area was clear."

"But the charge was ready, the wires attached and all that had to be done was to depress the plunger on the battery box."

"That's it."

"The high grass hid the battery box and the wires."

"Apparently. Why do you ask?"

I shrugged. "I'm just trying to remember. Certain things are still vague to me. After the explosion, what did you find?"

He lowered his eyes. "You were unconscious and badly hurt. There was nothing we could do for either your father or mother. I went to the edge of the quarry and saw the battery box dangling by its wires. Though the plunger was not all the way down, it was depressed enough to make the contact. It looked to me as if it had fallen off the edge and, in swinging free, the plunger must have hit the quarry wall and been driven into the box."

"Harley," I said, "if the wiring was attached to the lead-in passing to all the explosive charges, wouldn't that wiring have been blown to bits? So how could the battery box be dangling?"

"Some of the wiring to the box had been wrapped around the base of a small bush which didn't blow up."

"I'm sure you know the spot where I was found."

"Yes. I was one of the first ones there."

"I remember running to Mama and Papa. Was I close enough to where the wiring lay to have tripped over it?"

"Yes," he said somberly. "And, as I just told you, the box was almost at the very edge so any strong movement with the wire could have sent it overside."

I leaned forward in my chair. "Did my parents die because of my carelessness?"

He looked up in shocked amazement. "My God, no. It was an accident. A horrible one, true, but not the first we've had in the quarry, though the worst one. Nobody is blamed unless there's gross negligence. Certainly, such wouldn't apply in your case."

"I did it, unwittingly or not."

"Betty, don't start blaming yourself again. Believe me, you're innocent of any wrongdoing. If anyone should assume blame, it's Reggie or I."

"It's kind of you to say so," I said. "But I fear it's something I will have to live with the rest of my life."

"I hope, with time, the horror of the tragedy will fade from your mind."

"Thank you, Harley. I shan't keep you longer."

He arose and looked down at me. "I'd like to drop in more often, Betty, but I can't be casual when I'm around you and I have a feeling I'd be wasting my time."

"You would," I said. "I think of you as a friend

and as a trusted employee."

He reached down and clasped my hand lightly. "That's the nicest tribute you could pay me. Good night, Betty."

"Good night. Have a pleasant evening. I'm sure she's both young and beautiful."

He smiled agreement. "I wish you didn't know me so well. I might have a chance."

"You like it just the way it is. Admit it."

"All right. As of this moment, I'm a self-confessed rogue."

"A most appealing one, I might add."

I accompanied him to the door leading into the hall and sat there while Lorette saw him out. I motioned to her then to come into the den. She did so and, sensing an urgency from my manner, closed the door behind her.

"Lorette, please take a mantle from my closet—a warm one—and go to the stable. Have Chuck harness the buggy—it's the fastest. I want him to take you to Dudley Seaver's home. See if he's there. If he isn't, go to Dr. Egan's and ask him to come here as quickly as possible."

She regarded me with alarm. "Yes, Miss. Is there something wrong?"

"I don't know and I won't until you return. I pray God you'll bring back word Dudley is safe."

"At once, Miss." She went into my room and returned with a mantle.

"Put the hood on your head, Lorette. There'll be a chill in the air. And try to leave the house without anyone seeing you."

"Yes, Miss Betty. At once."

She opened the door leading into the hall cautiously, looked about and listened. Then, with a brief nod of farewell, she slipped through, leaving it slightly ajar. I wheeled the chair back to the fireplace, eager for its warmth. I felt chilled through, not because the room was cold, but it was almost as if I had a sense of foreboding. Of impending doom. I wondered if it could be Dudley's or mine. I was so engrossed in the morbid idea I didn't hear Maggie enter.

"I thought you'd send for me, Miss," she said, her voice a quiet reproof.

"I was comfortable and felt you might be resting," I replied.

"It's late, Miss. Wouldn't you like me to help you to bed?"

"I'm not tired," I said.

"You look it," she countered. "Or is something worrying you?"

"No, Maggie. Why don't you lie down on the couch?"

"Why don't you let me help you onto it, Miss?"

"I want to stay where I am. However, if you wish to retire, you may wheel me into the drawing room. I presume the others are there."

"They're not, Miss. The room is empty. I guess everyone is tired from their little expedition. Including myself, Miss."

"In that case, I insist you wheel me into the drawing room. You may rest here."

"I'll do no such thing, Miss. I'll stay right here with you. I favor the easy chair with the ottoman for my feet."

"Papa favored it also."

She settled herself in the chair, propped her feet on the ottoman and let her head rest against the softly cushioned leather back. I expected she'd close her eyes, but they remained open and seemed to fasten on my stiff form. I felt uncomfortable under her direct gaze, but I pretended not to notice. The tick-tock of the mantel clock, not even heard ordinarily, seemed deafening and a funereal stillness settled over the house. I didn't know if Maggie had heard the buggy leave. I hadn't, but I'd been so filled with concern over Dudley, I doubt I'd have heard anything short of a dynamite explosion.

Finally, Maggie broke the silence. "You're frightened over something, Miss."

"No I'm not, Maggie."

"You are, Miss."

"And if I am?" I countered, giving her a direct look.

"It's because of the dress, isn't it." She made it a statement.

"No. I'd forgotten about that."

Was her smile vindictive or did I just imagine it? "Which proves it was a dream."

"I suppose."

"You know. You got frightened, but it was just a dream. No one would save a torn, bloodied dress."

"Not unless someone wished to frighten me with it."

"And who would do that?"

"I can't imagine. Can you?"

"No, Miss." Her manner, which, I felt, verged on belligerency, again reverted to benignity. It was as if she realized she'd let down her guard and almost revealed her true feeling for me. Though I had no proof of her animosity toward me, I couldn't suppress the suspicion with which I now regarded her.

She settled back in silence, and, as before, her small, beady eyes never left me. It was as if I were her prisoner. I wondered what she would do were I to accuse her of being in my home in the role of a traitor or, perhaps, my gaoler.

FIFTEEN

I don't know how long it was from Lorette's departure to her return, but when she came into the den, my mantle on her arm, alarm was etched on her thin features, confirming her worst fears.

"Yes, Lorette?" I asked.

"Mr. Dudley did not return home, "she said.

"Oh, dear God, no," I exclaimed, tightening my grip on the arms of my chair so as not to lose control. I felt like screaming, releasing all the pent up apprehension I'd been filled with since her departure.

"Dr. Egan and Chuck have gone to the quarry to see if he's there," she said. "I'll hang up your cloak, Miss."

"Thank you, Lorette. How is Mrs. Seaver?" As if I didn't know, I thought wearily.

"Terribly worried," she called from the bedroom. "Mrs. Grenow is remaining with her until Dudley returns."

"I pray that he will," I said in an undertone.

Maggie's feet now rested on the floor and she leaned forward in the chair. "That's probably where he is, ma'am. In the quarry office, working."

"I believe Harley was the last one to leave," I said, disputing her statement. "Though I hope you're right."

"So do I, Miss."

When Lorette reentered the room, I said, "Please ask my aunt and my cousins to come down to the drawing room. Maggie, will you wheel me in there, please?"

"Glad to, Miss," she said.

When we were assembled in the drawing room, I told them of the mission I'd sent Lorette on because of my fears regarding Dudley. Needless to say, the three of them were shocked, yet none shared my horror. It was understandable. They were not living here when the dynamite blast went off, killing Mama and Papa. They'd not seen what happened to me the day Maggie—either through fear or deliberate intent—let go of the wheelchair after the explosion and almost sent me to my doom.

But when the doorbell pealed through the house and Lorette opened it to admit Jeffrey, I believe they knew my worst fears were realized. His eyes were still horror-filled with what he'd viewed. He came directly to me and squatted down before me.

"Dudley is at the quarry," he said, taking both my hands in his.

"There, you see, Miss, your fears were for nothing," Maggie said.

Jeffrey looked up at her. "He's dead."

Her face blanched. "What . . . what happened to him?"

"Apparently he fell from the top of the quarry," Jeffrey said.

"What was he doing up there?" Aunt Liz asked.

"I'd say he was on his way here," Jeffrey stated.

"And lost his footing," Lew reasoned.

"Perhaps," Jeffrey said.

"What do you mean by perhaps?" Lew prodded.

"I don't know," Jeffrey replied. "His features were mutilated almost beyond recognition. Still beneath him is a taffeta frock. It is soaking wet, as if it had been out in that drenching rain of last night and stuck in some airless place, preventing its drying. It's terribly soiled, but I believe the color is blue."

I covered my mouth with my hand to hold back the cry which almost escaped me.

"My God," Lew exclaimed. "It's obvious what happened. Dudley must have been the one who got in your room, Betty, and hung up the dress to frighten you."

"Why would he do such a thing?" I asked.

"I have no idea," Lew replied soberly. "But one thing's certain, you didn't have a nightmare last night. The way I see it is that he may have been hiding in the room and when you left it, he grabbed the dress and escaped through the window."

"But suppose he didn't," I countered, a little annoyed at Lew's glib acceptance of Dudley's guilt. "How did the dress get out of the room?"

Lew said, "Surely you don't think I threw it out the window."

I said, "I'm so horrified I don't know what to think. All I know is Dudley is dead."

Jeffrey said, "I sent Chuck to the village for the Constable and the undertaker. I'm the Medical Examiner in the village."

"Poor Mrs. Seaver has to be told," I said.

Aunt Liz said, "I'll go to her."

"So will I," I said. "To offer my condolences, for what they are worth and to assure her she need have no financial fears. I'll see Mr. Parnell in the morning and tell him to assume responsibility for her care. Also, to pay all funeral expenses and provide a headstone."

Maggie said, "Miss, I don't think you should go out in the night chill."

"I'm not an invalid, Maggie. There's no need for you to go."

The doorbell rang then, interrupting further talk. It was Harley. Lorette brought him into the room. Once he observed our faces, he knew something was wrong.

He addressed me. "I stopped by Dudley's to make certain he was home. When I learned he wasn't, I went to Reggie's. He was home, but swore he didn't see Dudley leave. I came back to tell you I'm going to the quarry now and see if he's there."

Jeffrey stood up. "There's no need. Chuck and I found Dudley. He's dead."

"What happened?" If Harley had an awareness of the tragedy, he was an excellent actor.

Jeffrey told him. He also mentioned the dress.

"What was he doing with a dress?" Harley asked.

"I think he panicked," Lew said, then turned to me. "Did you tell Harley what happened in your room last night?"

When I revealed I hadn't, he filled in Harley with the incident of the dress, adding, "We thought Betty had had a nightmare that seemed so real she actually believed that dress was in the room. Now we know it was."

"But how did Dudley get it?"

Rena spoke this time. "Lew thinks Dudley put the dress in Betty's room and when she became frightened and went for help, Dudley either slipped back into the room from the window or he was already hiding in the closet and he picked up the dress and got out the window again. Apparently he concealed the dress somewhere. Then, when Betty sent for him this afternoon, he became frightened. Maybe he realized she saw him."

"This is all supposition," I exclaimed. "We don't know that Dudley did any of that. The only thing we do know for certain is that he is dead." I turned to Lew. "Will you harness a carriage and take Aunt Liz and me to Mrs. Seaver."

"And me too, Miss," Maggie said.

"There's no need for you to go," I said.

"I think she should," Jeff said.

I didn't agree, for I didn't want this woman in Mrs. Seaver's home, but I knew he had a reason for disagreeing with me, so I acquiesced. Maggie gave a satisfied nod, as if she'd won a little victory and, indeed, she had.

And so we went to Mrs. Seaver's. It was sad news we brought, but she bore it stoically. Her courage was awesome to behold. I was quite helpless, being able to do nothing but sit. Mrs. Grenow was a comfort to her and so was Aunt Liz. She had packed an overnight bag and insisted on remaining with the two ladies. They seemed pleased she would do so and so was I. I took my leave then and Lew drove Maggie and me back to the Castle. Lew went directly upstairs, after being informed by Jeffrey everything had been attended to and Rena had already retired.

I insisted Maggie go in the den and lie down, for I wished the opportunity to speak privately with Jeffrey. Her eyelids were heavy and she gave me no argument, merely cautioning Jeffrey to waken her when he left. He promised to do so and, appeased, she went off.

He told me that Dudley's body had already been removed and that the Constable had returned to the village. He added that, though he considered Dudley's death an accident, he was puzzled by the dress. Jeffrey stated then that in all fairness he had to tell him about the incident of my wakening the night before and seeing the dress hanging from the window.

"Did you voice your suspicions regarding the deaths of my parents?"

"No," he replied. "Because they're just that—suspicions. We have no proof."

"True. But there must be proof of someone's guilt, somewhere. We've got to find it."

He told me then he'd looked in on Uncle Elijah, who was saddened by the news and couldn't believe Dudley was engaged in any wrongdoing regarding the quarry. I couldn't either, nor could I believe he was in any way guilty of what had happened to Mama or Papa, or had anything to do with my being near the cliff the day Maggie had wheeled me there and the dynamite explosion had taken place. To my mind, Dudley had been murdered and when Jeffrey and I were alone, I made that statement.

"I agree," he said. "Who knew you wished to see Dudley?"

"Only Lew and Rena," I said. "Though at the dinner table I mentioned it because I'd asked that he come here before he went home. When he didn't, I was perturbed."

"Someone is frightened," Jeffrey said. "I am too.

For your safety."

"I wonder how Dudley came in possession of that dress."

"I believe he was accosted on his way here after work and murdered. His body was hidden until dark. The murderer then threw his body from the top of the quarry, probably stuffing the dress inside his coat. When I found him, he'd been dead for several hours."

"And who got that dress out of my room?"

"Either the murderer or your cousin Lew threw it out the window."

"Oh no, Jeffrey. Not Lew."

"I'm not saying he did, but he had the opportunity to do so."

"But why? He didn't live here until after Mama and Papa died. He had no knowledge of the working of the quarry."

"Perhaps he caught a glimpse of the murderer through the window. He may have struck up a liaison or is intending to indulge in a little blackmail."

"That's so difficult to believe. Only this afternoon he mentioned being our European emissary to sell marble abroad."

Jeffrey looked bemused. "What?"

"He and Rena are celebrating their fifth anniversary next month. He told me she wanted a trip abroad, but he was in no position to give it to her. I told them it would be my anniversary gift to them. He refused pointblank to accept."

"Go on," Jeffrey prompted.

I told him then how Lew and I had decided on a way in which he could earn his anniversary gift.

Jeffrey said, "You know, you may have been lured

into that. I'm beginning to wonder if marble intended for certain clients is being diverted to other channels, probably even to Europe. Dudley may have known about it."

I remembered then Aunt Liz telling me of Papa's visits to Dudley before his death and I related the story to Jeff.

"Your father knew something was wrong," he commented. "He may even have known the guilty party. Chances are he did, but was waiting for the proper time to reveal him for what he was."

"Well," I said, "I can't keep you here any longer. You need your rest."

"You need yours far more than I," he said. "I don't like leaving you here unprotected."

"I don't think I'll be in danger for awhile," I said. "With Dudley's murder—and that is the only way in which I can refer to his death—the murderer may feel safe, at least for a time."

"True," Jeffrey agreed. "But be on guard every second."

"I shall, my love," I promised.

Our lips touched in a gentle embrace, then he wheeled me to the closed door of the den.

I said, "The quarry will be closed the next two days. Dudley's funeral will be the day after tomorrow. I suggested to Mrs. Seaver that some of the pallbearers be employees of the quarry. It pleased her."

"She'll not be able to attend the services," Jeffrey said.

"She knows that," I told him. "She wishes the cortege to pass the house. A last glimpse of her son who loved her dearly and was devoted to her." A sob escaped me. "I can't help it, Jeffrey. I feel so responsible."

"How could you?" he asked.

"I sent for him. The murderer feared Dudley might reveal that he knew and killed him."

"I wonder why Dudley didn't go to the authorities?" Jeffrey mused.

"Perhaps because he needed the work and if he couldn't prove his accusation, he'd be laughed out of town. Or if it wasn't that, perhaps he didn't dare for fear he might be killed. And once his income stopped, his mother would be destitute. She won't be though. I'll see to that. Papa had intended to do it, Aunt Liz told me, but he was apparently killed before he could attend to the matter."

Jeff was regarding the door. When his hand extended, I thought he was going to tap on it. Instead, he grasped the knob quietly, gave it a quick turn and pushed it open. It opened only an inch or so. Maggie cried out in surprise. Obviously, she'd been listening. I wondered just how much she'd heard.

"I was just coming to get you, Miss," she said. The color which suffused her face, plus the tremor in her voice, betrayed her sudden nervousness.

Jeff regarded her soberly. "I'll hold you responsible for Miss Betty's safety."

"Don't worry, Doctor. I'll see nothing happens to her."

"You'd better," he retorted, then turned and walked briskly to the door.

She brought me to my room. I made no attempt at conversation and neither did she. After she had me settled in bed, she said, "Would you care for a glass of milk to help you sleep, Miss?"

"No, Maggie," I replied with a sigh. "I'll sleep."

"I hope so, Miss."

"So do I," I replied and turned my head away from her. She put out the lamp and moved soundlessly from the room.

In the quiet and darkness of my room, I wondered if there would ever be an end to the tragedy that beset this house and the quarry. I prayed for the answers to the causes of such horrors and for a cessation of them.

SIXTEEN

The next morning Harley and Reggie came to the Castle. They were somberly garbed with dark suits and black ties. They told me they'd already called on Mrs. Seaver to pay their respects and offer their condolences. I wondered if either of them could have done that, in all good conscience, if they were guilty of Dudley's murder.

Rena and Lew hadn't yet risen. Aunt Liz was at Mrs. Seaver's so I invited them to breakfast with me. They accepted and Harley wheeled me into the dining room. I'd already excused Maggie and I imagined she was eating in the kitchen. She favored it whenever I didn't need her and I suppose it was because she and Gildy were acquainted with most of the villagers and it gave them an opportunity to indulge in a little gossip. I didn't mind, for certainly, Gildy's cooking didn't suffer because of it.

This morning, along with bacon and eggs, she served wheatcakes with maple syrup. I noticed Reggie's hand trembled as he held his fork. I didn't believe it was from nervousness. It could be from lack of sleep, though when he bent forward to bid me good morning, I detected a strong odor of alcoholic spirits. I didn't pay it too much mind though, for I knew there were men who held death in the same fear as the gentler sex. In his case, he probably needed to bolster his courage by indulging himself. His eyes were badly bloodshot and, as if aware of it, he never took his eyes off his plate. I was surprised that he ate so lightly.

"Don't you feel well, Reggie?" I asked.

"Oh, yes, Miss Betty," he replied. "It's just that what happened to Dudley has me badly upset."

"It has all of us," I told him. "Dudley was a very loyal employee. I know Papa held him in high regard. It will be so difficult for Mrs. Seaver. She and her son were a devoted pair."

"They were indeed," he replied.

"I've sent Chuck to the village to order a large floral wreath in the name of all the employees. There will be others from each member of our family. Since Mrs. Seaver wishes the cortege to ride past her house, I want her to know in what deep respect Dudley was held by his co-workers."

"I too sent a floral wreath," Harley said. "It was the least I could do."

"I'll do so when I get back to the village," Reggie said.

"There's no need to," I replied serenely. "I'm sure that what has been sent will cover the casket as it is driven past the house."

"Nonetheless, it's only fitting I do so," he said.

"I'd still like to know where Dudley got hold of your dress," Harley said.

"So would I, particularly since I doubt he'd ever seen it on me," I said.

"He saw it on you, Betty," Harley said. "Reggie, Dudley and I were the first three to reach the area of the explosion."

"But the dress should have been disposed of," I said. "It was in horrible condition."

"I was too concerned with getting you to the house to notice the dress," Harley said. "Do you remember it, Reggie?"

"I'm not much on clothes,' he replied. "Never took an interest in them. Either male or female."

His statement didn't jibe with what Maggie had told me, but I made no comment. They left shortly after, saying they would spend the day at the funeral parlor. I thanked them, telling them I would come there later in the day. And I did, along with Lew, Rena and Maggie. Of course, the casket couldn't be opened, due to Dudleys poor broken body and so the floral offerings helped to ease the grim occasion.

No word went out that there was the slightest suspicion of foul play. In fact, all I feared was that, since the Constable knew only of the incident of the dress, he might, in some way, feel that Dudley had been up to something illegal. It made me all the more impatient to learn how he'd met his death.

The funeral services were simple but touching. Reverend Blaine spoke kindly of Dudley who was a practicing member of the congregation. Lew carried me into the church and placed me in a pew near the front. I was greatly surprised when Mrs. Mandaray came in and sat next to me. She wore a purple silk frock which fashion had come out two years ago. It had a familiar look and then I remembered—Mama had one exactly like it in a garnet color. Indeed, Maggie had spoken the truth when she said Mrs. Mandaray had had Mama's clothes copied for her in a different color.

I had no further time to dwell on it, for the casket was brought in then. Jeffrey, Harley, Lew and Chuck were among the six. I noticed Reggie was missing. The fifth pallbearer was Mr. Yates, the undertaker and the sixth an employee at the quarry whose name escaped me.

While the services were going on, I became aware of the overpowering scent of lavender. I favored the scent, but with discretion. Now I had an almost constant urge to sneeze. Of course it was coming from Mrs. Mandaray and being a large woman, she gave off a lot of body heat which would make the scent more noticeable. And then, almost without realizing it, my head turned slowly and I regarded her with growing awareness, for I remembered my frock, hanging from the window latch, giving off that same overwhelming fragrance.

Could it be, I wondered, she had taken the dress? But she wasn't at the Castle. Then who? Reggie? And why? Why a dress of mine—particularly one torn, bloodied and soiled with dirt. And where was Reggie? Apparently the identical thought was passing through her mind for, from time to time, she kept looking at the back of the church.

And then the services were ended. Lew carried me back to the hack. Then the cortege, led by the hearse, drawn by four black-plumed, well-curried horses, started. It proceeded down the main street and paused for a few moments in front of Mrs. Seaver's house. She and Aunt Liz were in the window. Mrs. Grenow had been given leave to attend the services and she rode in one of the hacks I'd provided. I saw the two ladies touch their eyes with their handkerchiefs. Mrs. Seaver raised a hand as if in farewell to her beloved son. She gave a mere nod of her head as a signal to the driver and the procession continued to the cemetery. Naturally I could not go to the graveside, but I rolled down the window and listened to the simple prayer Reverend Blaine spoke. Then it was over. Over for Dudley for all time.

We stopped at the undertaker's and Lew transferred me from the hack to our carriage. From there, we visited Mrs. Seaver briefly. I knew Jeffrey would look in on her later. He'd told me so. She was bearing her grief with the same degree of courage she displayed in enduring her painful illness.

I was looking forward to seeing Jeffrey again. I wanted to tell him about Mrs. Mandaray and her idiosyncrasy about copying Mamas' clothes—also, her preference for the scent of lavender. Not that that, in itself, was unusual; only the lavishness with which she perfumed her clothes with it. Then I thought of Reggie and recalled his bloodshot eyes. Apparently, he'd imbibed too much and was unable to carry out his duty as a pallbearer. Could it have been, I wondered, a guilty conscience?

I hadn't long to wonder because we were no sooner home than Jeffrey arrived. His entrance was as brisk as it was two nights ago when he brought the grim news regarding Dudley and his features were as somber.

Rena, Lew, Maggie and I had just gathered around the table for supper. I'd already sent Lorette into the village with two baskets of food for Mrs. Seaver. Without a word to anyone, Jeffrey bent and kissed me. I might have been a little self-conscious about it, but I sensed the air of urgency about him.

"What is it?" I asked.

"Reggie Mandaray hanged himself in his attic. Apparently he did it this morning."

Lew's lips pursed in a soft whistle. "So that's why he didn't show up at the undertakers," Lew said.

"Why would he do such a thing?" I exclaimed in horror.

"He left a note—very brief. It said, 'I'm sorry. May God forgive me.'"

I addressed Jeff. "Please take me into the den."

"You haven't eaten, Miss," Maggie said.

"I couldn't," I said. "You stay and have your supper."

Lew arose. "I'll hitch up the buggy and go into town. I may be able to do something for Mrs. Mandaray."

"Please do, Lew," I said.

Rena said, "At least it didn't happen at the quarry. If it had, I'd go upstairs now and pack our bags."

Her statement was heartless, yet I couldn't redress her, for Dudley's death had had an adverse effect on each of us. Even Maggie was subdued. I think the picture of Mrs. Seaver in the window was what really upset us. It brought home the utter loneliness which would be her lot, but which she would bear with her usual stoicism.

"How is Mrs. Mandaray?" I asked.

"Very hysterical," he replied. "I gave her a sleeping draught. A next-door neighbor is staying with her."

"Good," I replied. To Lew, I said, "If there is anything I can do for her, please let me know."

"I will," he promised and left by way of the kitchen. It saved many steps.

Jeffrey wheeled me into the den and closed the door after I told Maggie she could have an hour to herself. Once we were settled before the fireplace, I mentioned, first of all, Reggie's suicide.

"How horrible," I exclaimed. "And what did he mean by asking God's forgiveness and stating he was sorry?"

"That's what we have to find out," Jeffrey replied.

I nodded. I told him then about Mrs. Mandaray's dress being identical to Mama's and how Maggie had told me Mrs. Mandaray had stated she had all of Mama's dresses copied by Mrs. Adams.

"And Mrs. Adams is rather expensive. But she's worth it."

Jeffrey seemed intrigued. "That is odd."

Then I told him about the overpowering scent of lavender emanating from her person, stating the dress hanging on the window had it to the same extent.

"She must have had that dress," he said.

"How did she get it?"

"I suppose Reggie, in some way, got it."

"But why would she want it?"

"She's an eccentric. Or worse."

"Do you mean—insane?"

He nodded. "Cleverly so. No one, not even a doctor, would suspect unless he was around her enough to observe her strange ways."

"Maggie said Reggie had a closet full of clothes also. They wore their extensive wardrobe only when they went to Boston, but they'd not gone since I returned from the hospital."

"Suspicion seems to point to Reggie, though I wonder."

"You mean he didn't hang himself? He was murdered—like Dudley?"

"No—he hanged himself. An overturned chair and the note removed any doubt of it. I was sent to calm Mrs. Mandaray. Harley got there after I did. He was stunned by the news. Genuinely so."

"Could it be a guilty conscience? When he came here yesterday morning with Harley, he showed the results of overindulgence in alcoholic spirits."

"We'll keep an open mind on it for the present. However, if Reggie wasn't alone in this, you must be more alert than ever."

"Don't you think I'm safe?" I said. "Two deaths in as many days?"

"The first was murder," Jeffrey said remindfully. "The second suicide. If there is still a murderer about, he may fear Reggie wrote another note."

"If only he did."

"I doubt it." Jeffrey spoke with such finality I gave up all hope. "I must go back now. Please take care."

"I will," I said.

He bent down and kissed me. "The circumstances of the last few days don't favor romance, but this can't go on. Pray God it ends this night. If Reggie was the murderer of Dudley and your parents and it was for that he asked forgiveness, then you have nothing to fear."

I nodded, but took small satisfaction in the statement, for Jeffrey didn't seem convinced. Yet there was only Harley left and I couldn't imagine him being involved in duplicity of any sort.

At the door he said, "I'll send Maggie in."

I nodded. "Good night, my love."

"Good night, my beautiful."

Maggie came in then and wheeled me into my room. I didn't demur, for I felt very weary. I'd even neglected to massage my muscles today and I recalled Jeff's warning about not neglecting it under any circumstances, for only in that way would they regain their tone. But I couldn't do it tonight. I just lay quietly in my bed. I didn't even want the lamp extinguished.

Two hours later, I still lay there and Maggie, seemingly disturbed, came in. "Could I get you a glass of warm milk, Miss?"

"Yes, please. And have one yourself."

"I will. With such horrible things happening, I can't sleep either."

When she returned, I reached eagerly for the glass. "Please put the light out," I said. "I'll sip it in darkness."

"All right, Miss." She set the tray on the bedside table, but picked up her glass. "I'll take mine in the other room, but I won't sip it. I need it to relax me."

"Good night, Maggie."

"Good night, Miss."

SEVENTEEN

I sipped my milk slowly and believe I'd only consumed about a quarter of the glass when I felt blessed sleep overtake me. I set the glass down on the tray and settled back on my pillows. I'd had Maggie close and fasten the window, for I had no wish for another night visitor—even an unseen one.

Yet it seemed as if I could hear the soft sighing of the wind, the rustle of leaves in the trees and an animal calling out. It was all so real. Now I could feel the night breezes and it came to me that I was not stretched out on the sofa, but seated in my wheelchair and I had no recollection of how I'd gotten there.

Yet I felt certain it was a dream. I had to be in my bed; Maggie was in the room beyond. There was no night breeze, no rustle of leaves. The sound of an animal was part of the dream fantasy.

But my eyes were open. I blinked them to make certain. I *was* seated in the wheelchair and I *was* somewhere in the open with the night all about me, dark and full of unknown terrors.

My first impulse was to scream, but I held that back and went about determining just where I was. There was a weird, bulky shape to my right, rising quite high and dimly outlined against a dark sky. For some reason it seemed menacing, until I realized this was one of the gadder machines. These monsters were used only on the floor of the quarry so that's where it must be.

But how in the world had I gotten here—and why was I here? I felt cold and wrapped my arms around my body, but still I shivered. Whatever the solution of this mystery could be, there was no time to dwell on it now. My fundamental effort must be to get out of here, to return to the warmth and security of the Castle. Later, I could try to figure out how this happened. But how could I possibly get back by myself? I couldn't. Yet I'd gotten here.

My eyes were growing more accustomed to the dark now and in the distance I made out the square form of the shed, used as an office by Reggie, Dudley and Harley. This was their headquarters and each had a desk there. If I could reach that—and manage to get inside—I would be protected from this chill air, at least.

I dropped my hands to the wheels of my chair, but I discovered the brake was on. I managed to dislodge that by the lever provided for that purpose and the chair began to move as I turned the wheels. It wasn't easy work because the floor of the quarry was not only uneven, but littered with pieces of marble, some of them quite large.

Something hit the marble floor with a crash. It landed some distance behind me, but it provided me with a definite scare. I thought it to be a piece of loose rock or marble. They sometimes fell like that.

Another crash was closer, but before I could wonder about it, a third hit not twenty feet from where

I sat in the chair. Then it was that I knew why I was here. I was going to be murdered. Rocks were already being hurled at me from the top of the quarry.

Here, at the bottom, confined to a wheelchair, I was a fine target because I couldn't move quickly and I couldn't see the rocks coming. No doubt whoever threw them from the edge of the cliff could see me, for I would be outlined against the light-colored marble. If I was only a darker blob of shadow in the night, it would still be possible to see exactly where I was and direct the rocks so one of them would eventually strike me.

From the way they smashed and splintered, throwing debris all about, I knew they were huge. I suddenly felt like someone trapped at the bottom of an enormous barrel while a murderer leaned over the edge and threw heavy objects at me. I was completely helpless.

A sob, like that of a trapped animal, escaped my throat as I wheeled the chair sharply to my left and gave the wheels a hard turn so that the chair shot forward a few feet. Just about where I'd been a large chunk of stone crashed onto the floor. As it splintered, it threw little pieces of the rock, some of them so sharp they must have inflicted tiny cuts in my skin.

I wheeled the chair again and purely on impulse I sent it rolling toward the wall of the quarry, not away from it. I hoped whoever sent those rocks crashing down would be convinced I'd try to roll my way off the quarry floor, not in the opposite direction where the wall would surely trap me.

It was a profitable impulse because half a dozen

huge rocks were sent crashing down all around the area where I'd been and would have been if I'd rolled straight ahead. But now I was deeper in the quarry. It would take longer to escape it, but I reasoned that I'd probably saved my life. For that moment, at least.

Just how long I could continue to save it was something else. Even with legs, I'd have been in grave danger. All I knew was an awful and growing terror. I couldn't get away. I was a cripple and I was doomed.

Never, in all the agonizing months of my being unable to walk, did I realize how dangerous such a handicap could be. Seated in this chair, incapable of swift or even stealthy movement, I didn't have a chance unless a great deal of good fortune favored me. With my chair almost touching the further wall of the quarry, whoever was trying to kill me now had but to drop his missiles over the edge and straight down. I couldn't stay where I was, for I had no way of knowing if I was a more visible target at that spot, or less.

I had to reach the quarry office. There the rocks could not hit and I'd at least have a door to lock if the murderer came down to finish the job. Also, I knew there was a gun in the office. Papa insisted one be kept there because this blasting and working marble and stone sometimes uncovered nests of rattlers and a gun was needed.

That gun now became the most important objective I'd ever known. I had to cross an expanse of quarry floor so wide it would take me three or four minutes traveling at the best speed I could get out of the chair. All the way, every foot of it, I'd be a target, and yet if I didn't take the chance, I'd soon be crushed to death by the resumption of the rock-throwing.

I had been near the quarry wall not more than half a minute until I came to this decision. In half a minute, the murderer could begin dropping his rocks, so I propelled the chair forward as fast as I could. Behind me, and not too far behind, a huge boulder smashed to bits against the harder floor of marble. I was again generously sprayed with fragments.

I kept the chair moving, shifting its direction every few feet so that I rolled along a zigzag path. Another rock came close, but not with the dangerous nearness of most of the others. Perhaps I was getting out of range now. I could feel my strength waning, in my arms and shoulders. But I'd been under a most severe strain and I was tiring. If I faltered now, all my efforts would have been in vain because I was convinced that once the murderer discovered he couldn't kill me with those rocks, he was coming down here to accomplish his purpose in an even more direct manner.

The wheelchair hit a slight slope and went faster. No more rocks fell. I kept going far beyond what I thought was the limit of my endurance. Then I was at the door to the shed. If it proved to be locked, I was lost.

It opened when I turned the knob. There was no raised sill to force the chair over so I rolled straight inside. Though it was dark, I knew about where the desk was located and, unless it had been moved, the gun would be in the bottom drawer.

I pulled the drawer open, but I couldn't see inside

so I rummaged through it, almost giving up hope when I didn't find the weapon. Then my hand encountered the cold, hard surface of the gun. It was a long-barreled six-shooter. I'd never fired a gun in my life, but this time I was going to do it.

I rolled the chair to the entrance of the shed. I listened a few seconds. I thought I could hear someone scrambling down the incline. I was sorely tempted to wait until the murderer got close so I might identify him, but that would be far too risky. I didn't know if I could hit the side of the quarry with a bullet, so I simply held the gun with both hands and pulled the trigger four times.

The gun went off, the sound of the explosion echoing and re-echoing through the quarry as if it had been from a cannon. I knew the sound of the shots would be heard at the house and the murderer would likely know that too. Besides, he must realize it was a revolver I held and that there were still bullets left in the gun. He would have no idea if I could shoot straight and he'd be unlikely to take a chance.

Despite my terror, I believed a murderer to be a coward. I sat there with the gun in both hands, waiting and trembling, because I knew now that even if a killer appeared before me, I'd never be able to shoot him, much less hit him. I had to depend on the threat of the gun to frighten him away.

After several minutes, there was a distinct sound of someone coming down the ramp. I tensed, preparing myself. I would shoot and trust the murderer to turn and run.

"Who's down there?" It was Lew's voice.

Relief flowed through me. "Lew! Come down quickly."

"Where are you, Betty?" he called back.

"In the shed. Hurry!"

He entered the shed at a run, but stopped abruptly when the light from his lantern revealed the gun in my hand. I set the weapon on the desk beside me. I was trembling and on the verge of hysteria. He came to my side and let his hand rest lightly on my shoulder.

"Was it you who fired the shots?"

I nodded. "Someone tried to kill me."

He looked at the gun, then his gaze flicked back to me. "How did you ever get here?"

"I don't know really. Someone had to bring me here. Whether I was brought in my chair I don't know. What I do know is that when I awakened, I was on the quarry floor, in my wheelchair. I was terribly bewildered, though not for long."

"What do you mean?"

"Someone at the top of the quarry started to throw rocks down, obviously in an attempt to kill me."

"Kill you?" he asked, still not convinced.

"Exactly," I said grimly. "Thank heaven I didn't panic. Otherwise, they'd have succeeded. I kept my chair moving and maneuvered it close to the wall, making it difficult for the murderer to aim at me."

"Who would want to kill you?" he asked.

"The same person who killed Dudley," I replied.

"Are you saying Dudley was murdered?"

"I am," I said firmly.

"And you think Reggie was murdered also?"

"No, but I thought he might have killed Dudley

and he couldn't live with the knowledge of what he'd done."

"What was Reggie up to?"

"If I knew the answers," I said wearily, "I'd not have found myself in this situation because the murderer would be behind bars where he belongs. Please take me back to the Castle."

"But if Reggie murdered Dudley, why would you still be in danger?"

"I don't know, but I am." I was fast getting impatient with Lew's inability to accept as factual the statement I'd made. "Please take me back."

"Of course, Betty." He got behind the chair and started wheeling it out of the shed. "Did you catch even a glimpse of whoever brought you here?"

"No. I didn't waken until I got here."

"Forgive me if I sound stupid, but I'm trying to understand how someone carried you here without your once awakening."

I spoke with sudden understanding. "Forgive me for being impatient with you, Lew. Of course, it's puzzling, but it's the truth. And I can think of only one reason why I didn't awaken."

"Please tell me." He spoke as he guided the chair around the shed and started up the path.

"I was drugged," I said.

"You mean you take medications," he said. "and something was put into what you took."

"I don't take a thing. But I did drink a glass of warm milk."

"That's right. I saw Maggie in the pantry when I came back from the village. Lorette was heating some milk."

"Was there anyone else in the kitchen?"

"Not that I saw. But then, the only other ones in the Castle are Rena and your uncle and Gildy, but she retires early."

I thought of the reason for Lew's journey to the village. "How is Mrs. Mandaray?"

"She was still resting. The lady staying with her said Jeffrey gave her enough sedative to keep her under until morning."

"I wonder how Maggie is?"

"She should be up. The sound of the gun awakened me. Rena's terrified. I don't know if your uncle was awakened."

"In case he was," I said, "please reassure him when you return. Jeffrey doesn't want Uncle Elijah coming downstairs yet."

"I will," Lew promised.

Once inside the Castle, we learned why Maggie hadn't been aroused by the shots. She was, in a deep sleep, snoring gently. Lew shook her lightly in an effort to waken her, but she only mumbled incoherently. I noticed her glass of milk was empty, while I recalled drinking only about a quarter of the glass of mine.

"Maggie sleeps as if she's been given a sleeping draught. Apparently I was also. Someone slipped it into our milk, but I drank just a little of mine. That's how I awakened. The night air helped to revive me."

Rena came into the room, her features tense with fear. "What happened?"

Lew explained briefly. "You have sleeping powders upstairs," he said. "I remember your buying them the other day."

"I didn't touch them," she replied. "The package is still intact."

"Will you check to make certain?" he asked.

She did so, returning with the box which she held out for our inspection. "There were twelve powders in here. There are now seven. Five are missing."

"I'm sure someone slipped the five powders into our milk," I said. "I have a faint headache."

Maggie groaned softly. Lew called her name and again shook her, more firmly this time. She opened her eyes, closing them quickly against the lamplight. She moaned a second time, then murmured, "Oh, my poor head."

She sat up and opened her eyes again, blinking them repeatedly to force them to remain open. It was an effort, but she managed.

"What's going on?" Her speech was slurred.

"Rena, please waken Lorette and ask her to make a pot of coffee," I said.

"I'll make the coffee," she replied. "No need to waken her."

I didn't argue, though I'd have liked to speak to Lorette. However, it could wait until morning. Maggie went into my bathroom and was gone a while. When she returned, she looked a little better and told us she had put cold, wet cloths on her brow. It was evident, for the water had spilled down the front of her wrapper.

Shortly, Rena brought in the coffee and Lew joined us in a cup. I told Maggie then what had happened to me.

"How can anyone get in here without waking me up?" she demanded, looking genuinely annoyed.

"We were drugged, Maggie," I said.

There was no doubting her stupefaction. "How could that be, Miss?"

"The milk was drugged."

"It couldn't be. Lorette heated it. She poured it too. I saw her."

"Nonetheless, it was. Give me your glass, please."

She handed it to me and I asked her to wheel me back into my room. My glass, still one-quarter full, was still there. I set hers alongside mine.

"These glasses are not to be touched," I said. I put the glasses on the table and set the small tray over them.

"What are you going to do with them, Miss?" she asked.

"I'm not sure," I said. "I just don't wish them disturbed."

I knew exactly what I intended to do—give them to Jeffrey when he came. I wanted the contents of the glasses analyzed. There was still a trace of liquid in Maggie's and covered, it would be less apt to evaporate.

"I'd like to get in bed now, Maggie."

"Miss, would you mind tellin' me again what happened?"

I did, but briefly. I knew she wasn't faking having been drugged, for her speech was still slurred and her movements were slow but I still didn't trust her.

"You can well imagine how exhausted I am from my ordeal," I said, when I finished my tale.

"I can indeed," she replied, stifling a yawn.

She was scarcely a help, for she had no coordination, so I shifted myself from the chair to the bed.

"Good gracious, Miss," she exclaimed in awe. "I had no idea you could do it."

"Why not? I did it the night my dress was hanging on that window."

"Of course," she replied. "I never gave that a thought. You'll be walking yet."

"I intend to," I said. I felt the time for subterfuge had ended.

"You mean you've tried?"

"I've not only tried—I've done it."

"I guess I won't be with you too much longer, will I, Miss?"

"Time will tell, Maggie. Time will tell."

"Yes, Miss. Good night, Miss. Glad you weren't hurt."

"Thank you."

She put out the lamp and I sank back on my pillows. My muscles ached more from tenseness than from having been used. I wondered if my life had depended on it, would I have been able to walk. I smiled then, at the irony of the thought. Hadn't my life been forfeit down in the depths of the quarry, yet not once did I think of using my legs to escape my enemy. It was as well. I'd managed without them and if I'd ever gotten up and fallen, I'd have been completely at the mercy of the killer.

I was surprised at the tap on my door. It was Lew. "Is there something I can do for you?" he asked.

I had a sudden inspiration. "Yes," I said. "I have a pair of crutches concealed in the mausoleum. Would you be afraid to go there and get them for me?"

"Certainly not," he said, though openly startled at the request. "What are they doing there?"

I smiled in the darkness. "I wanted to surprise you all—to stand up and walk unaided. But after what happened tonight, I think I'd better start using the crutches here so I'll be on my feet that much faster."

"You mean you've already walked?"

"Oh yes," I replied glibly. "No distance though."

"That's certainly news."

"Heartening, I hope," I said.

"Most heartening," he replied.

Rena addressed Lew. "You better go upstairs and tell Elijah what happened. He heard the shots and is very upset."

"Please go, Lew," I said. "He may as well know."

"Right away, Betty," Lew said.

I doubted either Lew or Rena were aware of Uncle Elijah's heart condition, but knowing how impatient he was, it would be wise for him not to remain in suspense any longer than necessary.

There was the sound of cups and saucers being placed on a tray and the voices of Rena and Maggie, lowered so as not to disturb me.

Maggie said, "I'll carry it out. You'd never manage it."

Rena said, "Thank you. Good night, Maggie."

They left the room together. Shortly, I heard Maggie return and close the door softly. That was the last thing I remembered.

EIGHTEEN

I was quite upset when I awakened and discovered the glasses gone. Maggie disclaimed responsibility, stating Lorette had come into my room and taken out the glasses without her knowing. Lorette, not realizing their importance and detesting untidiness of any kind, had removed them and was innocent of any wrongdoing.

I spent the morning practicing on my crutches. Maggie walked on one side of me; Lew on the other. I wasn't nervous and managed fairly well. Their amazement was something to behold. Rena came in a few times to observe my progress. She seemed intrigued as well as surprised.

"You keep a secret well, Miss," Maggie said.

I smiled. "I hadn't wanted anyone to know until I was able to toss these aside and walk. But I feel certain that will come."

"If it doesn't," Lew said with a smile, "it won't be because you didn't try."

It was mid-afternoon before Jeffrey arrived at the Castle. He went upstairs first to see Uncle Elijah, but was gone only minutes when I heard his steps pounding down the stairs.

I'd had a nap and was moving about the room

on crutches when he entered. Maggie excused himself, knowing she'd be dismissed anyway. Much to my disappointment, he didn't even seem surprised. Obviously, Uncle Elijah had informed him of what had happened to me at the quarry.

He greeted me with, "Thank God you had presence of mind enough to outwit whoever tried to kill you last night. Was the Constable notified?"

"I never thought of such a thing," I said.

"He should have been." Jeffrey's anger pleased me, for it made evident his deep concern for my safety. "I'll see him when I go back to the village."

"Must you leave?" I asked.

"Mrs. Mandaray is completely insane. I have her heavily sedated now and I've sent word to the next town where there is an asylum that she must be brought there. I have to go back and await their arrival. They have a special vehicle for such cases. I'm sorry to say she's become quite violent."

"The shock of Reggie's suicide apparently did it."

"It helped, but I imagine it had been coming on for some time. She wanted your dress. She kept calling it your party frock and kept referring to you as the little princess. Apparently, that's how she thought of you. Perhaps because the natives named this place Bowen's Castle."

"I wonder how Reggie got the dress. Apparently, he got it for her. She probably saw it at Mrs. Adams." I shuddered. "It was stained with blood."

"She wouldn't see that. She just saw the beautiful frock. She probably envied both you and your mother. She wanted lovely clothes."

"Maggie says she has them."

"She has. Closets full. Reggie could never have

afforded them on his income."

"Could he have been the employee not to be trusted?"

"It would seem so," Jeff stated. "But don't forget you were attacked after his suicide. When I return, I'll bring your aunt with me. There has to be someone here you can trust."

"I beg of you, Jeffrey, not to bring her back. She may be in danger."

"So are you," he replied.

"I think not," I said and really believed it. "I imagine, by now, whoever is behind this must realize I'm indestructible."

"But you're not," Jeffrey contradicted impatiently. "I can't, in all good conscience, leave you here behind."

"Yes, you can," I said.

"Only if you'll promise me you'll not leave this room until I return."

"I promise."

"I don't think anyone would attempt to harm you in the Castle."

"I don't either."

"I'll return tonight as soon as possible."

"I'll be waiting impatiently."

"I'll also notify the Constable of what happened to you last night. This has to stop."

"I agree. Have you seen Mrs. Seaver today?"

"No, but I will on my way back here."

"Thank you, Jeffrey. Tell her I'll pay her a visit tomorrow."

"I'll bring you," he said, bending forward to kiss me. It was brief, but it bespoke our love for one another.

After he left, I napped again, not waking until supper. No one at the table talked very much. It was as if we sensed something ominous was about to happen. I wondered just how much of the courage I'd displayed to Jeffrey was real and how much false. But I'd resolved not to be a burden to him and that was why I wouldn't return to the village with him. However, I was frightened. Terribly frightened, for I didn't know whom I could trust in this house. I was suspicious of everyone and ashamed of myself for being so, though I managed to maintain an outer calmness that gave no evidence of my inner turmoil.

It was eight o'clock when Maggie brought me in a note. There was nothing on the envelope other than my first name.

I took out the slip of paper. It contained just one sentence. It said, "Darling, have Maggie bring you to the mausoleum at once." It was signed Jeffrey.

I was heartened to hear from him and told Maggie to take me there.

"At night, Miss?" she asked, looking apprehensive.

"Are you afraid?" I asked.

"Yes, Miss."

"Then call Lew, please. I'm sure he'll take me there."

"He and Miss Rena went for a drive."

"At night?"

"Yes, Miss. They said they were going in to see your aunt. Lorette gave them a basket of food to take."

"I'm glad," I said. "Will you go to the stable and ask Chuck to come here?"

"He drove them, Miss."

"Why wasn't I told?"

"I don't know, Miss. They didn't tell me. I just happened to see them go out the door."

"Then I'll have to wheel myself there."

"Oh no, Miss. You can't go out there alone."

"Dr. Egan wishes me to go to the mausoleum. I am going there."

"Why didn't you say so, Miss? I won't be afraid, knowing he's there."

"Give me my shawl, please, so we can get started."

She did so and slipped a cape around her shoulders. We started out, not pausing until we came in sight of the monument. Dim light flickered from it.

"There's nothing to be frightened about, Maggie," I said. "Dr. Egan has lit a candle. Its light makes the marble angel look taller than ever."

"It does, Miss," she said excitedly. "It does. It's beautiful."

"Do you really think so?" I asked.

"I do, Little Princess," she said. "I do."

"I asked you not to call me that."

"Mrs. Mandaray always called you that."

"Mrs. Mandaray is insane."

"She hated you and your mama, Miss."

"Why?"

"Because you had everything."

"She had it too, didn't she, Maggie?"

"Yes, Miss, she did. Reggie saw to that. And so will I have it soon. After you're gone."

I kept my voice calm, though sudden fear shot through me. "Do you hate me, Maggie?"

"Don't hate you nor like you."

"Please wheel me closer to the mausoleum."

"I'm wheeling you right into it, Miss."

And she did, propelling me faster and faster. I

turned to look up at her. In the faint candlelight, I saw her face contorted in hatred. She never looked down at me, just ahead at the tomb, but her twisted mouth looked evil.

I could see into the mausoleum now, but Jeff was nowhere in sight. I opened my mouth to scream, but fear paralyzed my throat. Then I saw the mausoleum door, fashioned of bars, was wide open. Maggie pushed me inside so violently the chair crashed against the further wall. Before I could even turn around and plead with her, she had stepped out and slammed the great door shut and promptly disappeared.

I sat there, frozen in terror. There was no sound now. A candle, set in one of the brass sconces beside Papa's niche, flickered fitfully, for there was a mild breeze and it came down through the opening where the roof would have been in an ordinary mausoleum.

I could see a thousand stars twinkling down and I wondered how much longer I'd see them, or anything else. I heard a scraping sound above me and when I looked up again, I saw a shadow moving. I could see the back of the angel, towering so high above. Suddenly I knew. The angel was going to fall backwards. It was exactly the right size to fill the mausoleum and it was positioned so it couldn't miss the opening. It would crush to death anyone inside the tomb. There was no escape because the ton or more of weight would occupy ever inch of space. I recalled Jeffrey commenting that the angel seemed tilted. He was right. It had been tilted to fall on me.

I began to scream. That was all I could do, except try to turn the wheelchair so I might reach the door. It was impossible. The confines were too narrow to allow the chair to make the turn. The door behind me could have been open for all the good it would do me, unless I could propel myself backwards.

This I did, and struck the iron barred door. I twisted around. The inside latch was missing. It had been removed so anyone inside would be unable to escape. I had seconds left, I knew. Whoever was on top of the mausoleum was now working faster.

I managed to turn myself around in the chair, to actually kneel on the seat. I reached up, grasped the bars of the door and then I pulled hard, drawing myself toward the door while the chair twisted slightly and then slipped out from under me and I was standing, clinging to the bars. I saw the outside latch handle and I reached for it.

Frustration lent added horror to my predicament. I found my voice and screamed for help. I clung with one hand now, my arm through the narrow spaces between the bars, my fingers barely touching the latch.

"Harley!"

The voice came fron the darkness outside. I saw someone move out from the tree line. It was Jeffrey. He shouted Harley's name again.

Then his shout became a cry of horror. "No! Harley . . . I'll shoot! Don't!"

A light flared briefly. Jeffrey raised the gun and fired as he ran. He reached the door, turned the latch, pulled the door open. All this in a matter of five or ten seconds. Someone moaned. That came from above me. Then I was in Jeffrey's arms and being carried. Something crashed down inside the tomb. As Jeffrey sped for distance, I could see that it was Harley. The candlelight revealed that much.

Apparently he was wounded, for he tried to get up, then to crawl. Atop the tomb, there was a muffled explosion. Jeffrey came to a stop. With me cradled in his arms, we watched the angel slowly fall backwards while Harley's screaming grew more and more intense.

There was a horrible crash as the angel hit the inside of the tomb and broke into pieces. Harley's scream was cut off abruptly. The candlelight was out. From the tomb now came a mist of fine gray marble dust. I thought I heard a woman's scream of terror, cut off abruptly. It was Maggie.

I said the first thing that came into my mind. "What was the explosion?"

"Harley set a small explosive beneath the angel which sat atop the mausoleum."

"So it was he who lured me there with the note."

Jeffrey said, "Open your eyes, my darling. Don't be frightened. You're safe. No one will ever harm you again."

What a blessed relief to find when I raised my lids that I was in my own bed. "Maggie?" I asked.

"She tried to escape from the Constable. She fell over the side of the quarry. No one could survive that."

"Lew and Rena?"

"They're packing. Going back to her parents. It was he who doped your drinks, yours and Maggie's. Harley wanted her doped too, believing it would look more convincing. Lew also threw your dress out the window that rainy night and it was he who carried your wheelchair to the quarry. Harley carried you, then went back up and threw rocks down on you. Lew doesn't know Harley was killed in the explosion, but he was. Lew believes Harley has talked, so he confessed his involvement, brief though it was. He also told everything Harley revealed to him. When he finished, I gave him a choice of getting out immediately or confessing to the Constable."

"I'm glad you did."

"I felt in view of what he'd told me, he was entitled to his freedom."

"What's that?" I asked.

"Harley, as you know, was an expert in explosives. He told Lew that the wire you tripped over, did not set off the dynamite explosion. If it had, there'd have been no trace of the wire and you know there was. The explosion was set off elsewhere. Harley knew your father walked along the edge of the quarry each day and had placed dynamite there. He had your father under surveillance and he set off the explosion which killed your parents and injured you. Afterward, he fastened the end of the broken wire to a bush, let the plunger box dangle over the side of the cliff, making it seem as if you'd set it off by tripping on the wire, sending the box overside to strike against the quarry wall. He also placed a small charge of explosive beneath the angel atop the mausoleum. I was right when I made the observation that the angel seemed to have a slight tilt to it. A pity I didn't examine it then."

"When did Lew get mixed up in it?"

"The night Harley hung your dress on the latch. Maggie opened the window for him after you were asleep. She also closed the door to the adjoining room. Lew told me she worked for Harley."

"How did Lew get mixed up in it?"

"The night you sent him in here for your dress, he saw Harley climbing back in the window to retrieve it. Lew brought it over to him. Harley told him to deny he'd seen it. Lew, not being stupid, knew Harley was not all he seemed and realized he'd hit upon a perfect situation for being counted in on whatever scheme was afoot."

"Foolish, foolish Lew," I said. "I'd have given him anything he wanted."

"I believe, more than anything, he wanted Rena's self-respect. Perhaps he thought her eyes would not wander so much, if he were financially independent."

I smiled. "Did she make eyes at you?"

He pushed my hair away from my brow and kissed it. "She's the kind of woman who'd make eyes at any man."

I sobered. "Was it Harley who killed Dudley?"

"We'll never know for certain, but I'm inclined to think it was Reggie and he couldn't live with himself afterward. It may be Harley ordered him to do it. Certainly, Harley knew of the existence of the dress and that Reggie's wife had it. That's another thing we'll never know—how it got into their hands."

"Was Harley stealing funds?"

"That and diverting marble to channels other than where they were supposed to go. That is, he sent inferior marble to the places which placed a *bona fide* order and the better stuff, he sold abroad. That was what Lew was after. He was a fool though. Harley would have gotten rid of him in some way. Harley wanted it all. Reggie was in on it too. Dudley wrote that he caught Reggie going through Harley's desk one night. It was after that that Reggie and his wife branched out in expensive clothes. Their home is furnished expensively also."

"Just what did Dudley write?" I asked.

Jeffrey bent down again and this time kissed the tip of my nose.

"Dudley kept a diary. I stopped in to see Mrs. Seaver as I promised you I would. Your Aunt Liz found it among his possessions. Your father and Dudley talked at length about Harley's guilt. It's all in the diary. Also, Reggie's, but with the latter, they lacked proof. Of course, neither your father nor Dudley had ever been in Reggie's home, or they'd have realized he couldn't have purchased such furniture, or lived as he did."

"Poor Dudley," I said.

"Yes," Jeffrey said. "He wrote in his diary he was afraid to speak out because if he lost his job or was murdered, his mother would be destitute. He wrote that your father had told him he would see that, because of what he'd uncovered regarding Harley—and, as I said, it's all in the diary—neither he nor his mother would ever want. But your father and mother were killed in the explosion before he could attend to that matter. Dudley also stated in his diary he believed the explosion at the top of the quarry was not an accident. That the wires had been so placed because your father walked there each day. Your father had already told Harley he was to be dismissed."

"Did Dudley make any reference to Maggie in the diary?"

"No. I doubt he was aware of her duplicity. Obviously, Harley fired her with a desire for further revenge, plus a promise of money. And now, my darling, you must rest. The Constable will wish to speak with you when you waken and so will I. To ask you to be my wife. The sooner, the better."

"May I consent without waiting to be asked?"

"That's what I like—an aggressive young woman. Also, one filled with courage and completely innocent of any carelessness regarding the death of her parents."

"I love you, Jeffrey Egan," I said.

"And I love you, Betty Bowen," he replied. He bent forward and, this time, our lips sealed our troth.

All that happened a year ago and Jeffrey and I have been married almost that long. I'm walking now. Perhaps a little stiffly and haltingly, but I've discarded the crutches. My beloved says that, with time, my stride will be as brisk as his. I hope so, but even if my leg muscles don't completely regenerate, I feel as if my recovery is quite satisfactory.

I did write to the good Dr. Beardsley—first to apologize for being such a difficult patient. Then to tell him of the wonderful progress I'd made, thanks to the ministrations of one of his former students, namely, one Jeffrey Egan. Dr. Beardsley replied, stating he would use my case—with my permission (which I promptly gave)—as an example to other patients who were as filled with discouragement and self-pity as I had been when I was under his care.

We have a new general manager at the quarry. He is completely trustworthy and most eager to discuss all facets of the business with Jeffrey and me. I've taken quite an interest in it because Jeffrey, being a dedicated doctor, devotes endless hours to his patients. Just now, he is at a neighboring farmhouse to help a woman deliver her firstborn. I am impatient for him to return so he can tell me how the new mother fared and how beautiful the baby is. I'll want to know in detail for, in a few months, I will present my beloved with a baby—boy or girl, it won't matter. If a boy, he will be named John after Papa; if a girl, Clarissa, after Mama. We want a large family, so Bowen's Castle will ring with the laughter of children.